MORE BY TH

THE TSCHAAA

Book 1: The Gathering Storm
Book 2: The Tsunami
Book 3: Typhoon of Steel
Free Range Protocol: Tales of the Tschaaa
Beyond the Great Compromise: Tales of the Tschaaa
Survivors: Escaping the Tschaaa

ANTHOLOGIES

Unnerving: Monstrosity
Unnerving: Descent
Unnerving: Wicked
The Mighty Pen
Unconditional
Cascadia
Tales of the Slug
Super: Unexpected Heroes Arise

BLUE FLASH

It Begins (The Why Files)
Dragons and Drugs (The Why Files)
Predators and the Press (The Why Files)
Felines and Marriage (The Why Files)
Love is Blue (The Why Files)
The Gentleman and the Tiger (The Why Files)
The Island (The Haunting of Orchard House)
Shane (Angels of Anarchy)

COLLECTED WORKS

Inhumanity: A Year of Stories

JADE EYES

MARSHALL MILLER

BLUE FORGE PRESS
Port Orchard, Washington

Blue Forge Press is the print division of the volunteer-run, federal 501(c)3 nonprofit company, Blue Legacy, founded in 1989 and dedicated to bringing light to the shadows and voice to the silence. We strive to empower storytellers across all walks of life with our four divisions: Blue Forge Press, Blue Forge Films, Blue Forge Gaming, and Blue Forge Records. Find out more at www. MyBlueLegacy.org

Blue Forge Press
7419 Ebbert Drive Southeast
Port Orchard, Washington 98367
blueforgepress@gmail.com
360-550-2071 ph.txt

This book is dedicated to all the Special Agents and Law Enforcement Personnel I worked with over some thirty years in my career of Protect and Serve. This is especially true with the last group of new and upcoming young agents and other "cops" I worked within my ultimate duty office in Seattle, Washington. You all demonstrated a new level of motivation and professionalism needed in today's trying times.

This story is also dedicated to all the victims of smuggling and trafficking, both human and animal. Humankind needs to do better in following the Golden Rule.

ACKNOWLEDGEMENTS

Of course, this novel would not have been completed without the understanding and support of my loving wife, Sheri. Our four furry family members were also patient with my late-night writing forays and provided me the occasional slurpy kiss to remind I was loved and appreciated. I love you all.

Without the support of my current publisher, Blue Forge Press, *Jade Eyes* would not have seen the light of day. Thanks again for your tireless support to an old dinosaur.

I hope all the readers enjoy this tome based on my actual occurrences and experiences.

JADE EYES

MARSHALL MILLER

TIGER, tiger, burning bright
In the forests of the night,
What immortal hand or eye
Could frame thy fearful symmetry?

In what distant deeps or skies
Burnt the fire of thine eyes?
On what wings dare he aspire?
What the hand dare seize the fire?

And what shoulder and what art
Could twist the sinews of thy heart?
And when thy heart began to beat,
What dread hand and what dread feet?

What the hammer? What the chain?
In what furnace was thy brain?
What the anvil? What dread grasp
Dare its deadly terrors clasp?

When the stars threw down their spears
and water'd heaven with their tears,
Did He smile His work to see?
Did He who made the lamb make thee?

Tiger, tiger, burning bright
In the forests of the night,
What immortal hand or eye
Dare frame thy fearful symmetry?

William Blake. 1757–1827

1.

The two dozen young Asian women and girls were huddled together in the far corner of the metal shipping container. Dressed in the most rudimentary of clothes; shorts, blouses and flip flops on their feet, it had been some time since any of them had showered or bathed. Their untended body odor mixed with the smell of vomit and overflowing human waste buckets. Several sobbed as the Chinese Snakehead smuggler swung open the large metal door and yelled into the container which sat on the back of a semi-trailer. The man clambered up the temporary wooden steps and entered the container, still yelling in Mandarin.

"What is all this crying and noise? I told you to be quiet or else." The average-build Chinese male then produced the "or else" from inside his belted loose legged trousers. He had made his own version of the traditional Cat O' Nine Tails from a section of broom handle and strips of cheap leather. The women cringed from the knowledge of what could come next.

"They're dead," a female voice rang out. Then several slender feminine arms and hands were pointing at two prone figures concealed in the shadows near the front entrance of the container. The Snakehead, cursing, produced a small flashlight to augment the single light bulb suspended from the roof of the shipping container. His flashlight revealed two small figures, still just considered girls as they had not yet reached their sixteenth birthday. He cursed louder as he saw they were not moving.

"Lee Chin, what's all the noise? What is wrong?" The voice resonated with the tone of one used to command, of being kowtowed to in his daily life. Before the Snakehead could formulate an answer in his now panicked mind, a figure ascended the steps and entered the container. He looked toward Lee Chin, who began a panicked stutter.

"Th-th-the two girls, here, Boss..." He still had his flashlight illuminating the two bodies.

The Boss, dressed in a tailor-made dark suit with silk shirt and tie, carefully knelt down by the two bodies in the detritus on the container floor. He tried not to soil his suit nor his highly shined shoes as he examined the motionless girls. With an expert touch, he felt the necks for a pulse and swore. Slowly the nearly six-foot-tall slender but muscular Chinese man known as the Boss stood up. He produced a silk handkerchief and wiped the fingers he had used to check the pulses one at a time.

"They are dead," said the Boss as if he were discussing a menu at a restaurant.

Lee Chin panicked. *"It's those North Korean dogs we got. They must have done something to them. I said we should never have agreed to smuggle North Korean sluts. They are nothing but trouble and very ugly."*

A female voice in Mandarin Chinese resounded

from the group of cowering females.

"*No. He lies. It's the food he brought. It made them sick.*"

The Boss turned his head lazily and looked at the source of the comments. A young and attractive Chinese girl nearing womanhood was standing out from the huddled mass. She stood with her head held high as if daring someone to try and break her spirit as she pointed to a makeshift table.

The Boss looked where the young female was pointing and saw some dishes, pots, and cans. He strode over and looked at the remains of a meal. His nose wrinkled in distaste, and he bent over and picked up an unopened can from a box on the floor. The Boss looked at the rusty and bulged lid. In one quick and fluid motion, he rifled the can at Lee Chin's face. Somehow the Snakehead flunky raised his left arm up far enough to absorb the can rather than have it smash into his face. He howled in pain.

"*You worthless pile of pig shit,*" the Boss hissed at his injured henchman as he approached. "*You pocketed the money I gave you for food and supplies, and then went American-style dumpster diving behind the Asian businesses, didn't you. Didn't you?*"

"Boss, I, I, I, I'm sorry. I was just trying to save us money..."

The open hand slap resounded like a pistol shot, and Lee Chin stumbled back, almost falling from the force of the blow.

"*Us? You talk of US? As if we are partners? Why would I partner with pig shit?*"

"*Please, Boss.*" Lee Chin tried to bow and kowtow to the Boss. "*I'm sorry! It will not happen again.*"

"*That's true,*" the Boss said. With one smooth motion, he pulled a chrome-plated Tokarev pistol from an inside the waistband holster of his suit pants and shot the Snakehead underling between the eyes. The high-velocity bullet made a thirty caliber-sized hole as it entered, and a more massive exit hole as the projectile tumbled sideways while transfixing the brain. Pieces of brain matter, skull, and blood splattered the walls of the metal shipping container. The now two-legged piece of meat flopped to the floor, blood flowing from the ruined head.

The Boss spit on the body. "*You pig fuck! I spent my time and treasure in bribing Chinese officials and Yankee round eye barbarian longshoremen at the Port of Seattle, to get my merchandise here, at the warehouse, in secret. And then, let a piece of shit like you damage it, or damage my operation? I think not.*"

The Bosses three bodyguards had dashed up the temporary wooden steps at the sound of the gunshot, weapons drawn. Two ethnic Chinese plus one large and stocky Mongol, none were as tall as the Boss, who was a bit tall for most Chinese.

"*Clean up the bodies,*" the Boss snapped.

"*Where do you want them, Boss?*"

"*Give them to our new friend, Sir Kahn. He will dispose of them for me.*"

At the name of Sir Kahn, the two ethnic Chinese men paled a bit. The stocky Mongol flashed a feral grin.

The Boss looked over at the young Chinese girl, woman, (it was hard to tell her age in the poor light and dirt). He beckoned with his left hand as he put his pistol away, used the fingers down method many Asians preferred, opening and closing his fingers into his palm.

"*Come here,*" he ordered. As she did, the Boss noticed his suit jacket, silk shirt, and tie were spattered with the dead Snakeheads blood. He cursed, this time in English.

"Shit. Even in death, the pig causes me problems." He looked up at the Chinese female.

"*Well, hurry up,*" he said in Mandarin. "*I do not like to waste time.*"

As she approached, the Boss could tell the young Chinese female was very attractive despite the poor light and dirty clothes. Jet black below shoulder length hair which she had somehow kept combed and brushed framed a pretty Chinese face with clear skin. Somewhat high cheekbones and a lovely, feminine nose by Chinese standards were displayed to the Boss as he produced his own small flashlight. He also noticed that her eyes did not seem to be the typical dark brown. Then he saw why they were special. They were green.

"*You have pretty green eyes. What is your name?*"

"*Lin Daiyu.*" She looked straight at him when she answered. No bow, no kowtow.

He tossed his soiled suit jacket at her and began to strip off his silk shirt and tie. She caught the coat but still glared at him.

"*Your age,*" the Boss asked. Daiyu did not answer.

He wadded up his shirt and tie and tossed them at her face. As she went to catch them, he stepped in quickly and grabbed her left ear. A quick, harsh twist and he had her on her knees.

"*There are two paths we can take, Lin Daiyu. One is the path of pleasure, the other is of pain. Now, your age!*"

"*Turned sixteen yesterday,*" she replied through tears of anger and pain.

The Boss grunted. She had fire, intelligence, and beauty, he thought.

"You would be of marriage age at the beginning of the last century." He paused, letting go of her ear. She grabbed it and rubbed it, now no longer meeting his gaze with defiance. He put out his hand. She took it, and he helped her up.

"I think my green-eyed lovely, that I can groom you for better things."

The Boss turned to his three bodyguards, who were supervising other flunkies to get the three dead bodies out of the container, and barked out orders.

"When you are done, take Lin Daiyu to the limo. We will take her to Madam Chou's Massage Parlor and have her cleaned up." He looked at Daiyu. *"No, you will not work there, my jade beauty. Hmmmm. Jade in English. A nice new name for you. One we can provide identification papers for easily."* The Boss paused for a minute, took her right hand, and kissed it.

"If you are as intelligent as I think you are, I think I can provide some challenging work for you beyond giving so-called happy endings," the boss said with a smile. *"That is if you promise to cooperate, not run away."*

The Boss squeezed the hand of the young woman—now known as Jade—hard. *"You will not run away, will you?"*

"No, Boss. I will not," she answered without delay.

"Good," he said. Then he smiled again. *"Once you get to know me, and I you, I'll let you know my name."*

He released her hand, looked up at the Asian women still clumped together in the corner of the shipping container. He sighed before he spoke.

"Now I must arrange for decent food and clothes

for your comrades. Something Pigshit should have arranged before this.

He looked into Jade's beautiful green eyes. *"Here in Seattle, good help is often hard to find."*

2.

FEDERAL DISTRICT COURT
SEATTLE, WASHINGTON

Your Honor, I would like to recall Special Agent Kim Kupar to the witness stand." Assistant U.S. Attorney Jay Bell's voice rang out as Kim stood up, waiting for the final word from the judge that she would be allowed to testify once again.

"Fine, Counselor. She may retake the witness stand." District Judge Wendy Yamashita peered over her eyeglasses at Kim as she spoke. "You are still under oath, Agent Kupar."

"Yes, Your Honor," Kim said. Her back straight with the hint of military bearing her Uncle had helped her achieve years ago, made her way to the witness stand near the judge's bench. Dressed in a dark navy blue women's business suit with a dress, jacket, white blouse, navy blue cross over bow tie and matching two-inch heel shoes, with jet black hair in a tight bun, Kim hoped this outfit projected the image of calm professionalism for which she strove. She knew her Punjabi, and Argentine mixed heritage made her seem very exotic. Her slight permanent tan and tall model good looks sometimes make people think "erotic" instead of exotic, made them dismiss her as just eye candy.

As she sat down in the witness stand, while Jay Bell shuffled his papers about, her mind flashed back to her last week of Investigation and Customs Enforcement/ Homeland Security Investigations Special Agents Training at the Federal Law Enforcement Training Center in Brunswick, Georgia. Senior Special Agent Rachael Williams, a senior instructor there, had invited all the graduating female Agents out for a "Girls Night Out" at Pam's Number One, the advertised largest and one of the oldest federal law enforcement and cop bars on the East Coast. Judging by the number of class memento T-shirt, organization patches, photos, old badges and "trophy" sets of men's boxers, briefs and women's bras and panties that adorned the walls and ceiling, Pams could at least lay claim to the largest number of LEOs served over the years.

"When you're a woman in law enforcement, you are always being watched and appraised," Rachel had begun after receiving her second drink. "I'm not just saying its only men that are checking you out, but also many of you so-called Sisters of the Shield, fellow female cops. They will, men and women, see you and size you up as potential competition as well as if you are going to be good back up in a fight, can you be trusted. Plus, everyone will watch your demeanor in professional situations like testifying in Federal Court."

Rachel took a sip of her drink—Scotch on the Rocks—then continued. "So, Ladies. Dress up too flashy, with a skirt deemed as too short or a blouse too tight and they will call you a slut behind your back, say you are trying to sleep your way to the top. Dress down too much, wear pants, slacks, rough shirts all the time, maybe try and be too much "Macha," you may soon be seen as a frumpy pain in the ass. Or, worse, as a man-hating dyke."

The dark-skinned African American woman took a more copious draught of her Scotch, spoke again. "Before some of you report me to the P.C. Police, I am not saying this is right. I am saying it *is*. These attitudes exist. I know. I'm forty-five, have had a badge and a gun since I was twenty-two. So, I saw it, lived it, felt it. If I offended you, so be it. You're on your own."

She finished off her drink before continuing. "Being a large and opinionated black woman didn't help me much either. Now, who's getting the next round? Because it sure as Hell isn't me."

Kim's mind snapped back to the present as AUSA Bell approached the witness stand and began to question her.

"Now, Agent Kupar, you testified yesterday on your findings upon completing a forensic examination of the substandard wiring harnesses supplied by the defendants and sold to the U.S. Government. Correct?"

"Yes, Sir." Kim looked at the Jury as she answered, making eye contact with the jurors.

"After your testimony, counsel for the Defendants, Mister Zhang and Mister Wu of China East Import and Export Company, said they would agree to stipulate the equipment was faulty and substandard, isn't that right?"

"Yes, Sir," answered Kim.

"Your Honor." Defense Counsel Louise Lassiter stood up, her voice loud. "May I ask why the AUSA is rehashing old ground? I object if he is trying to beat my clients up over a stipulation, we agreed to in the name of fairness, speed, and efficiency."

Lassiter was an experienced Defense Attorney, more so than AUSA Bell. And she let everyone know it. But the bright-haired blonde had already been taken down a notch by Judge Yamashita for her overly flashing and foxy clothes she liked to wear in court. Kim had overheard a quick admonishment from the judge, a very experienced jurist, that the courtroom was not a night club, so dress accordingly. Judge Yamashita was a Japanese American and former AUSA. Those people who had the unfortunate stereotype in their mind that she may have been a small and quiet Asian woman were soon reminded that she was a District Judge, who knew and felt the power she wielded. Such a reminder was not a pleasant one, either.

Judge Yamashita looked over her eyeglasses at Jay Bell again as she spoke.

"The Defense has a point. Cut to the chase, Counselor. I would like to put this case to bed by the end of the week, not the month. Do not try my patience by rehashing stipulated evidence."

"Yes, Your Honor," said Bell as he shuffled his papers a bit, swallowed as he stood in front of Kim.

"Agent Kupar, did I ask you last night to review the shipping and U.S. Customs documents of the numerous transactions and shipments involving the equipment in question?"

"Yes, Sir, you did," said Kim.

"And what new evidence or facts did you discover

in the additional examination?" asked Bell.

"That the translations from Mandarin by both the Government and Defense translation services were incomplete, and missed some salient points."

Lassiter jumped to her feet, again with a loud voice. "Your Honor! What is this? An attempt at sandbagging? We have the transcripts from—"

"Counselors, approach the bench." The judge had her eyes fixed on Bell as she spoke, and he began to sweat. It was unfortunate that he had a young-looking freckled face which seemed to scream "newbie" as well as the fact he blushed easily. As they were all close to the witness stand, Kim had no trouble hearing and seeing the conversation.

"Please tell me why, Mr. Bell, yesterday, when we all agreed to accept the Defense and Governments Chinese Translation transcripts as stipulated evidence because they were near identical, we should suddenly throw them out? Where and how did these discrepancies suddenly appear?" Judge Yamashita's eyes bored into the young attorney as she questioned him.

"Your Honor. I'm not asking to throw anything out," the AUSA answered. "Agent Kupar just discovered some notes in Mandarin jumbled up among the documents..."

"Mandarin?" Lassiter verbally jumped in. "Since when is Agent Kupar an expert in Mandarin? She doesn't look Chinese."

The hard stare of the judge switched from Bell to the Defense Counsel in a flash. Her voice came across hard.

"Careful, Counselor. I don't look like I should speak English as my primary language, either. But I do. I speak Japanese as an afterthought. So, watch your racial stereotyping."

The blonde attorney blushed. "Sorry, Your Honor, I didn't mean..." She tried to finish her comment. Bell saw this as an opportunity to jump in.

"Your Honor, please let me present the evidence and let the jury decide as to Agent's Kupar's abilities." Bell spoke as quick as he could without stammering. "After all, you have stated many times that you believe in the ability of the jury to see through what you called bovine excrement. You made these statements in some of your speeches given to law schools' graduating classes."

Kim saw a hint of a smile on Judge Yamashita's face.

"Ah, a young lawyer checking up on the ole judge," the judge said with the barest hint of a smile. "And just hung me on my own petard. Okay. Step back to your tables, please. I need to do a little grilling if I am to accept Agent Kupar as an expert in Mandarin."

"Ladies and Gentlemen of the Jury," the judges voice rang out. "I plan on ascertaining if Agent Kupar is sufficient of an expert in the Mandarin Chinese dialect as to be able to testify about supposed omissions and discrepancies in the official translations already accepted as evidence. As I believe in a totally informed jury, I plan to do this in front of you rather than in camera. That is if no one has an objection."

Both Defense and Prosecution answered in unison. "No, Your Honor."

Judge Yamashita turned toward Kim. "Okay, Special Agent Kupar. What languages do you speak fluently?"

"Punjabi Dialect, Mandarin Chinese, Spanish and English, Your Honor," answered Kim, firm and decisive.

"Hmmm. Quite impressive. Do you have proof or a form of certification of your abilities?" asked the judge.

"Yes, Your Honor. AUSA Bell has my official Homeland Security Investigations Language Proficiency Testing Results. I took the tests to qualify for additional proficiency pay." Kim knew her answer would elicit a request for the documentation, which the AUSA had at his trial desk.

"Counselor, the documents, please." Bell approached at the judge's order and handed the requested forms to the judge.

District Judge Yamashita's eyebrows raised a bit. "All Fives, which I know is the highest proficiency language ratings your agency give," she said. "How were you exposed to all these languages?"

"I learned Spanish, Punjabi, and English from my parents," answered Kim. "My Father ensured that my brothers and I all learned Mandarin Chinese, Your Honor."

"Why Mandarin?" asked the judge.

"My family owns a high tech and computer equipment company. My Father has done extensive business with the Chinese. He wished all his children would follow in his footsteps and work with him. Thus, as China was the fastest growing economy, we learned Mandarin." Kim's answer was to an oft-asked question, due to her fluency in such diverse languages.

Judge Yamashita again smiled a bit as she intoned. "Yes. Fathers often have plans for their children that have to be changed. Now. Proof that you can speak and read it here."

28 JADE EYES

Judge Yamashita turned to the official court Mandarin Translator, who had been completing a running commentary of the proceedings via their earpieces to the two defendants.

"Miss Liu," said Judge Yamashita. "Please ask the Agent a question or two in Mandarin."

"Yes, Your Honor." In Mandarin, Miss Liu asked Kim, *"You are a Federal Agent?"*

"Yes, Ma'am. I completed my training about a year ago." Kim answered without a pause.

"That is a nice business suit you are wearing," stated Miss Liu. *"Where did you get it?"*

"At Macy's, used to be the Bon Marche, in downtown Seattle," answered the Agent. *"It was on sale."*

"You look nice in that color of blue," opined the Translator.

"Why, thank you, Miss Liu."

The District Judge broke in. "Sounds like Old Home Week between you two. So I take it Agent Kupar speaks good Mandarin."

The Translator's eyes widened a bit as she answered. "She speaks Mandarin like a native Chinese. Better than some who grew up speaking Cantonese dialect."

Judge Yamashita turned back to Kim.

"What did you talk about?" She asked.

"My job, my clothes, Your Honor," Kim again answered without hesitation.

A few chuckles were heard in the courtroom and jury box, which the judge ignored.

"Well, Counselors. Any questions?" Yamashita asked.

Louise Lassiter stood up to speak. "I still have a slight problem, Your Honor, with the timing. Especially in light of all the problems, even the FBI is having with their forensics. First, the original Case Agent disappears, is not available for cross—"

"Objection, Your Honor." Bell interrupted. "Is the defense implying that we are involved in some Machiavellian ploy to confuse—"

"Wouldn't be the first time the Government tried to shore up a weak case—" began the Defense Counsel.

The judge slammed her gavel down.

"Enough! No bickering," she ordered with a loud and firm voice. "You," she pointed the gavel at Lassiter. "Know that Senior Agent Swenson was called away on a family emergency. I don't think he would lie to this court about his wife almost dying in childbirth just to get out of cross-examination, Counselor."

Now the judge was glaring in anger at the Defense Attorney as she continued. "You also agreed with the AUSA to continue on as you both said you wanted a speedy trial. So quit with the attempts at conspiracy theory."

"You," now she pointed at Bell with the gavel as she continued. "Get on with the questioning. I think Agent Kupar has demonstrated her ability to be certified by me as an 'expert witness' when it comes to Mandarin. But if this is a bunch of bovine excrement—" The judge let the end of the comment hang.

"Yes, Your Honor," the AUSA said as he began to collect his papers once again.

Kim looked at Lassiter. Dislike was turning into anger. Senior Special Agent Matt Swenson was her mentor, her Training Officer. He and his wife Pat had become close friends, Kim had babysat for their two other children. So for Lassiter to even imply he would be part of some government shenanigans caused her to boil. Matt was not that much older than Kim, she had just turned thirty. But he had years on her in experience, having started in Cyber-smuggling right out of college. He was a whiz with computer forensics.

Bell approached Kim in the witness stand.

"To continue, Agent. You once again reviewed the documents as per my request."

"Yes, Sir," she answered

"What did you find that was apparently overlooked?" asked Bell.

"On page three, on exhibit D-22. There is some Chinese calligraphy in light handwriting that was overlooked," Kim answered. "Here." She pointed to a specific spot.

"May I show the Jury, Your Honor?" Bell asked.

"Yes, go ahead," said the judge.

Bell walked over and pointed to the area on the page. Then he walked and let Lassiter peruse what he had pointed out. Wu and Zhuang began to whisper to each other in Mandarin.

"And what does the Chinese calligraphy state?" asked Bell

"It specifically uses the term '*Laogai*,' a Mandarin word that the Chinese Government uses to denote prisoner labor," answered Kim. "Also used in conjunction with the '*Kuli*,' which in English we know as 'Coolie.' Then it goes on to talk about frustration with the end product they were producing."

Judge Yamashita interrupted. "Counselor, we need to know what exactly was said. Word for word if you are trying to enter her testimony in as evidence."

"Yes, Your Honor," answered Bell as he looked at Kim. "Go ahead, please."

Kim collected herself. *Here goes*, she thought, then spoke. "It says, quote, ''These pig shit *Laogai Kulis* couldn't make anything that works if their lives depended on it. Wu, make sure the Yankee Dogs do not notice this shit.' End quote. Then the equivalent of two sets of signatures in calligraphy symbols. One Zhuang and the other by someone known simply as Boss."

Neither Wu nor Zhuang were much older than Kim, which begged the question in her mind as to how they were the supposed co-owners of the substantial business. And they had so far exhibited a disdain for anything 'Not Chinese,' looked at America as barbarian central. Thus, it was no surprise when Zhuang jumped up and began yelling at Kim in Mandarin. The U.S. Marshals Security Officers were quick to react, as Zhuang knocked Lassiter back while she tried to calm him.

"Order in this court," Judge Yamashita called out as she banged her gavel.

Kim stood up in an automatic desire to 'get involved, back up' any law enforcement action.

Zhuang then made the most unfortunate act of trying some Kung Fu move on the Marshals. He ate the Defense's table with his face, blood spurting from his smashed nose. Other Marshals from nearby rooms came busting in.

"*Order in the court!* Marshals, restrain that man." The judge yelled out as she turned toward the court interpreter. "What was he yelling?" The interpreter blanched, stuttered.

"You. Agent Kupar. What was he yelling?"

Kim took a breath, then replied. "He yelled that I am a half breed slut who should have been fucked good and hard by someone. Then I would not be here spreading lies in front of an old wrinkled and inferior Japanese woman whose crotch is dry and nasty."

Everything froze in time. Then, Judge Yamashita acted, her voice firm and icy.

"Marshals, get the Jury out to their Jury Room. Clear the Court Room of everyone else. Handcuff Defendant Zhuang there. We are about to have a short discussion here with the Defendants and their Counsel."

"Your Honor—" Lassiter started to speak, and the judge cut her off.

"Silence until the courtroom is cleared and secure."

Judge Yamashita then noticed Kim was standing, on edge.

"About to jump in, Agent Kupar?" she asked.

Kim blushed a bit as she answered. "Sorry, Your Honor. Training and..."

"And you were never raised to be a shrinking violet," the judge added and chuckled.

A couple minutes later and the only people in the room were Marshals, defendants, lawyers, the judge, and Kim.

"Stand Mr. Zhuang up." The Marshals complied with the judge's order, blood from Zhuang's broken nose staining his expensive suit coat, shirt and pants.

"Mr. Zhuang. You are in Contempt." The judge's voice rang out through the courtroom. "And I do believe the young AUSA will consider Assault on Federal Marshals charges based on the ill-advised attempt to strike my courtroom security officers."

"Yes, Your Honor," replied Bell.

"Judge Yamashita—" Lassiter started to say.

Judge Yamashita verbally cut her off. "Ms. Lassiter. I highly suggest you quickly confer with AUSA Bell here and your clients about a deal. I don't think anyone can erase what just happened in the eyes of the jury. If you want to file an appeal later, go for a mistrial, have at it. But the evidence this young Agent was testifying about will not go away. Which I believe will show criminal knowledge and intent concerning the sale of the substandard parts."

"Your Honor, we did not even get to the part about related deaths and injuries—" Bell began to say.

"That can be part of the deal-making," said the judge. "I'm now going to my chambers. I'll return in thirty minutes. Then I will call the Jury back in. This Court is temporarily in recess." Judge Yamashita banged the gavel and made her way to her chambers.

Kim walked out of the courtroom with a grinning AUSA Jay Bell. He was almost giddy as he spoke.

"Man, do I owe you, Kim. You managed to piss those guys off so much Zhuang lost it. Now, them agreeing to Criminal Negligence Charges that led to serious injury and death. No more trial, no jury deliberations which could have gone sideways." The young lawyer straightened his tie, tried to stand straighter. Kim, in her two-inch heels, was a bit taller than he was, and he seemed to be preparing to ask her something important.

As he was about to speak, Kim heard a familiar voice behind her.

"Ma'am." James Dean, the judge's clerk, walked

up. "Judge Yamashita would like to see you for a moment. She is in her chambers."

"Of course, Mr. Dean."

"I was about to ask you out to lunch," a disappointed Jay Bell stated with a frown on his face.

"Raincheck, Counselor. I promise," answered Kim.

"I'll hold you to that," Bell stated as Kim turned to hurry toward the Judge's Chambers.

Kim was glad Bell's attempt at lunch had failed. He was younger, straight out of law school and kept watching her with puppy dog eyes. Although he was nice, he did nothing for her. Him having the hots for her would just lead to frustration on his part. Best anything along those lines did not even start.

Kim knocked on the door to the Judge's Chambers.

"Come in," Yamashita said.

Kim entered, a bit sheepish as she found her voice. "Your Honor. You wished to see me?"

Judge Yamashita, now sans her robe and in a nice woman's business suit walked toward Kim with her hand extended. She had a smile on her face as she spoke. "Special Agent Kupar, I have not been in the business of the 'Feed and Care of New Agents' since I was an Assistant U.S. Attorney. I don't want to be considered playing favorites with the Prosecution, but today was something special."

"I was just doing my job, Your Honor," Kim said as she shook the judge's hand. As she did, she saw on the judge's Glory Wall a Certificate awarding a Black Belt in *Gojo-Ryu* Karate to one Mary Yamashita. The judge must have noticed a hint of surprise on her face as she glanced at where Kim was looking.

"Oh. That." The judge smiled again before she spoke. "Like you, I didn't always follow my father's wishes."

The judge turned back. "Young Lady, I may want to use your excellent language skills again if I get jammed in court with translations. Yes, I'll clear it with your bosses. People with your language skills are hard to find."

"Thank you, Ma'am." Kim Replied. "I was glad it all worked out."

The judge laughed, then continued. "I am glad also. Contrary to what some believe, District Judges like a little bit of change and excitement. You caused it today. Keep up the good work, young lady. Here."

The judge handed her a business card. On it were the words Professional Women in Law Enforcement, followed by a telephone number.

"Local group, lots of cops and lawyers," said the judge. "I'd think you'd enjoy attending a meeting."

"Thank You, Your Honor." Kim felt a bit on Cloud Nine.

"Job well done, Agent," said, Judge Yamashita. "Now, please take off. Don't want the Defense screaming about favoritism. Though I have to say, Ms. Lassiter grates on my nerves."

As Kim left the Judge's Chambers, a big smile on her face, her cellphone beeped that she had just received a text. It was from Agent Dennis Spain in the main office

"Return ASAP. Big meeting. Big Changes."

Kim frowned. Just as she was getting used to things. She sighed. Well, as the Chinese Curse said, "May You Live in Interesting Times." Things were shaping up along those lines with a vengeance.

3.

The Federal Courthouse in Seattle, Washington, was within walking distance of the Special Agent in Charge (SAC), Homeland Security Investigations (HSI) office. Thus, Kim hot-footed it to the office building on Second Avenue. The elevator up some twenty floors, and she used her crucial secure keycard to enter the front area. The receptionist, Betty Freedman, smiled at her and motioned to the main conference room.

"They're all in there, Kim," said Betty.

"Thanks, Ma'am." Kim used a rapid stride to enter the back of the conference room, hoping to sneak into a seat at the end of the table. No such luck today.

"Ah. Agent Kupar. Glad you could make it." Special Agent in Charge (SAC) Thomas Gill greeted and smiled at her as she tried to sneak in.

"Sorry, Sir. Court—"

"No need to explain, Kim. I just received a congratulatory call from a certain District Judge. She also twisted my arm to use you when she is short court interpreters." He turned to the Deputy Special Agent Brad Ball. "Did I miss something in her training records from FLETC?"

"Might have, Tom," replied Ball. "They have a tendency of burying things we may find useful under a bunch of touchy-feely crap."

The two Senior Supervisors were nick-named Mutt and Jeff. For Tom was tall, blond and imposing, and Brad was as short, stocky, and dark as the SAC was the opposite. They were a definite study in contrasts. But together, they made one of the best teams in Homeland Security.

Kim began to blush a bit, though her permanent tan skin color helped to cover. She quickly sat down, saw there were just short of a dozen other Special Agents as well as Assistant Special Agent in Charge Tim Weiss and Group Supervisor Dave Salmon. Weiss had a reputation for being a hard but fair manager. Salmon was eaten up with the Short Man's Syndrome and seemed to have a problem with women which he worked hard to conceal, sometimes. Salmon being here did not bode well in Kim's estimation.

"Well, Ladies and Gentlemen," the SAC began. "I'll make this short and sweet, then turn it over to the good ASAC and Group Supervisor. We in ICE, and here in Homeland Security Investigations, in particular, have had a unique situation fall in our laps. Thanks to some major screw-ups by our 'friends' in the FBI, our management has decided to push the envelope and expand the Department of Homeland Security's Forensics ability.

Specifically, those SAC offices who feel they have the potential in staffing and expertise will be given the chance to form local forensic units and laboratories. And not just in Cyber Crimes. I mean in all the traditional forensic sciences."

This set off a bit of murmured surprise among those seated. Tom Gill allowed his message to set in before he continued.

"Thanks to people like Senior Special Agent Matt Swenson, we have an expertise in Cyber Crimes and Child Pornography investigations second to none. Now, I plan to expand on that."

He looked directly at Kim as he spoke. "I understand you have a degree in the biological sciences as well as having taken some forensic pathology at your University. Is that true?"

Kim tried not to stutter and blush as she replied. "Yes, Sir. I thought about Zoology or being a Veterinarian at one time. The forensic classes aimed me toward law enforcement instead."

The SAC chuckled. "Well, some zoo's loss is our gain. You're in as you have a strong background in lab sciences, can help the rest in finding their away around that environment."

Tom continued. "The rest of you either have backgrounds in Cyber Crimes, Human Trafficking, Smuggling, or some exposure to the human sciences. For, let's face it, people. We deal both with merchandise and humans crossing our borders. Why not do our own lab forensic work?"

A loud voice piped up. "Why me, Boss? You need an old border rat around a lab? I don't do mazes."

Rex Moyer was most certainly the oldest person

in the room, within a year of Mandatory Retirement. Kim looked at the burly brown-haired man with a handlebar mustache sitting a couple seats away. Known to many as T-Rex, because he was such a 'Dinosaur,' from the old school of Border Agents, he was not known for having any background in the hard sciences. Unless it was the science of putting bullets on target. Tom Gill had known Rex for years, and there was a level of mutual respect. Even though Rex probably added to his gray hair count over the years.

"Mazes?" replied the SAC. "I have trouble getting you to put your statistics and time in the computer. You're too stubborn to do mazes."

This lead to a round of laughter in the room. Rex took this in good stride, as he took pride in this 'stubbornness'. Especially when it came to pointing out that Management was about to really screw something up.

"Actually, Rex, we need some of your corporate memory and Southwest Border smuggling experience," Gill stated. "Not to mention your contacts in the International District."

The SAC glanced at his watch, then finished his briefing. "Alright. That is the basis. ASAC Weiss and Group Supervisor Salmon will flesh out the details. Bottom line, this office *will* be at the cutting edge of making the Department of Homeland Security the other thousand-pound gorilla in the room. Good luck."

Tom and Brad Ball left the conference room, and everyone looked at Tim Weiss.

"You all know me," the brown-haired and fit man said. "Do your job, you'll have no trouble. But expect this new Forensics Investigation Group to be work. Hard work since we are having to start from scratch. We need to work together. Clear?"

Everyone nodded or murmured assent.

"John here will give you're your specific marching orders. Talk to you all later." Sam rose and left. Salmon turned with a sour look on his face to the working Agents. He began to toss packets of papers and forms to all the Field Agents.

"Here are the standard procedures and draft instructions for you," Salmon grumbled. "They are both from D.C. and management here. Follow them."

Salmon glared at the assembled federal investigators and support personnel, then continued.

"I did not ask for this assignment. I expect to be transferred to Headquarters any day now. So, if you screw this up for me, I will screw things up for you. Understand?"

Moyer made a rude noise that seemed to emanate from someone else. Salmon glanced angrily around and then fixed his eyes on Rex. The elder statesmen Agent gave him his best shit-eating smile he could produce.

"Here, T-Rex!" Salmon said as he tossed a substantial training file at him. "Until Matt Swenson returns, you're Kupar's Training Agent."

"Hey. I don't know anything about lab science—" protested Rex.

"You're senior. You got picked. Don't like it, retire now." Salmon said it as a challenge.

Rex Moyer swore under his breath and took the folder. He stood up. "Latrine time I think. Coffee goes right through me."

Salmon glared at Kim before he spoke to her.

"Remember you are still in Training Status, Agent. I don't care how many degrees you have. Follow orders. Now, get to work." With that, Salmon stood up, walked out as fast as he could.

Rex beat everyone else out the door and disappeared. Kim made her way back to her cubicle and desk. She felt excited and apprehensive at the same time. Excited that he could use her knowledge and specialized background to good use in this new assignment. Apprehensive because she knew some 'eyes' were now watching her closely. Not just Salmon but other Special Agents. She remembered what Rachael Williams had told her at the Academy about 'Whack a Mole' office politics.

"Stick your head above the group," the black Senior Agent had stated. "There is always someone who will enjoy whacking you back down to their level. Some people cannot stand other's success, so they screw up the mission. Pathetic egotistical bastards."

Now Kim knew her 'mole' head was sticking up.

"Hey Kim," Dennis Spain said as he stuck his head into her cubicle. "Want to go to lunch?"

She smiled at her good friend. Dennis was a dark-skinned and Lothario-handsome black man with a touch of Hispanic heritage. She and Dennis had hit it off the first day she had met him in the Seattle SAC Office. He'd been on the job for almost three years, coming off a failed attempt at being an NFL Linebacker.

"Too small, they said. But not fast enough to be an 'End.' So, Uncle Sam got me." Dennis had said with a grin. He was just over six feet tall, so Dennis was not exactly small. However, 'small' and 'large' in the NFL apparently meant something different.

"Yeah, sure," replied Kim. "Just let me put these files away—"

"Sorry, Handsome. Training Officer dibs." It was Rex speaking, coffee cup in one hand, Kim's file in the other. "You got your G-ride in the garage?"

"Yes, Sir."

"Good. You drive, I direct. Let's go."

As Rex turned and walked off, Dennis gave Kim a shrug and 'What can you do' look.

"I saw that Spain. I have eyes in my butt, remember?"

"Brown eyes, right?" Spain shot back.

"Yep. You nailed it. Coming, Agent Kupar?"

"Yes, Sir," Kim replied as she grabbed her vehicle keys.

As she caught up with Rex, without looking at her, he asked, "You have your assigned firearm, right?"

"Yes, Sir," she replied. "Attached on my hip, with my spare magazines, cuffs, collapsible baton."

Now Rex looked at her. "Hmm. Your suit there is well-cut. Conceals your stuff—I mean, equipment."

Kim looked back at him as they reached the elevator. "I study and examine how things work," she said. "How to do my job right, Senior Agent Moyer."

Rex grunted a reply. "Scientific Method?"

"Yes, Sir. Works outside the laboratory also."

They entered the elevator, and Rex waited for her to push the floor button.

They rode the elevator in silence, then went to the parking garage. All Special Agents had a Take Home Government Vehicle, a 'G-ride,' as they were on call twenty-four hours a day. Of course, the junior Agents received the older vehicles. Kim had an older and well used Ford Mustang ICE/HSI had obtained when some county or state police agency had a cut in funding. It was designed as a pursuit vehicle, with a small trunk and back seat. Trying to transport prisoners was a bit of a pain. But the V-8 engine meant it could go like a raped ape if needed. As Rex folded himself into the passenger seat, he gave it the once-over.

"This 'Stang held up well," the Senior Agent opined. "You like it?"

"Yes, Sir. Nice acceleration."

"That it does have," stated Rex. "Now, head out and on to Seconds Avenue. Then, south to the International District, what used to be called China Town before the P.C. Police came along."

Kim glanced at her new Training Officer and spoke. "I thought it was because Japanese, Vietnamese, and Koreans began moving in."

Rex looked back at her. "Hey, how long have you lived here in Seattle?" He asked.

"About five years, Sir."

"You're just a newbie. Trust me. I know the history. Seattle is my home town." Rex stated with authority. "By the way, been to the 'Jade Garden' on Seventh?"

"Yes, Sir. My father has business meetings there."

"Huh. I guess you aren't a complete newbie."

Five minutes later, Kim had the luck of finding a parking spot near the Jade Garden. Rex seemed moderately pleased, though Kim was still unsure about his gruff exterior. Was he always this way, or was it an act for the "Newbie"? She missed Mathew more every minute. They walked into the crowded restaurant, it being lunchtime in a popular eatery.

"Jade Garden is one of the oldest operating Chinese restaurants in Seattle," Rex said. "I've been eating here for years."

An older Chinese woman yelled at Rex from behind the cashier position. Smaller than some Chinese but not tiny, the woman made a beeline toward the Senior Agent, began speaking rapidly in somewhat accented English.

"Agent Rex! You eat here again, but not with your wife." The woman winked at Kim. "I know she is not a mistress as your Jeanie would remove your manhood if she caught you."

"Now Mother Bao..." The woman was not much older than Rex, but he referred to her as an 'Elder' who demanded respect. Before either could continue, Kim bowed enough to show respect to an elder woman and greeted her in Mandarin.

"Madam Bao, it is a great pleasure to meet you. My father has often used your restaurant as a place for business meetings with clients."

Mother Bao's eyes widened a bit to hear a clearly non-Chinese greet her in her native tongue. She looked at Rex and said in English, "She speaks Mandarin like a native. Where have you been hiding her?"

The woman turned toward Kim, took her hand and bowed, slipping back to Mandarin once again.

"Who is your father, my dear? I know almost everyone who comes here."

"Balraj. Singh Kupar. Of Kupar Electronics and Computer Imports."

"Ah, Yes! He comes here often. But I didn't realize he had a daughter."

Kim smiled as she replied. *"Since I did not follow in*

the family business, nor provide grandchildren yet, he sometimes forgets I live nearby."

"Never!" Mother Boa exclaimed, "A good father never forgets their daughter, no matter how much they may irritate them. Your name is—"

"Kim, Ma'am."

Rex took this moment to insert himself back into the conversation.

"Well, now that I understood about every tenth word, how about speaking in English, so I don't feel like such a third wheel? I was never one who picked up languages quick."

Mother Bao grinned and slapped Rex on his arm. "Quit lying," she scolded. "You speak Spanish quite well. And your Mandarin accent is getting better."

Kim's mouth formed into a wry smile as she switched to English. "So he is learning Mandarin—"

"Hey, what I do is my business," Rex shot back. "Now. Mother Bao, is there such a thing as a quiet, private area here. I need to discuss some matters with new Agent Kupar here."

"For you, Agent Rex, of course," the Chinese woman answered. "Follow me."

Mother Bao was soon pushing her way through the lunchtime crowd, speaking loud and in rapid Mandarin as she ordered staff out of the way. She led Kim and Rex to a secluded booth in the back corner that had just been vacated. Rapid-fire Mandarin again and the used dishes were whisked away, table washed down and a table cloth placed on the table-top, all in record time. Mother Bao turned to Kim and spoke in English.

"I will bring you a special meal, Kim Kupar. No need to order or to pay."

"Ma'am," replied Kim. "I can't accept. I'm on duty."

"Don't be rude, Newbie. Just take it," Rex stated in an adamant tone.

Kim looked at her Training Officer. "I thought taking gifts due to our position—"

"Cultural and Ethnic Relations. Leave a big tip if you are worried about the ramifications, Kupar," Rex instructed. "Unless you start taking cash in envelopes, I've got you covered."

Kim nodded, not wishing to argue. She could tell that the Senior Agent was set in his ways. Stubborn could be his middle name. The sat down as hot Chinese tea was brought. Kim poured them each a cup as Rex pulled out what could only be her personnel and training file and began perusing it after putting on some reading glasses. She sipped her tea as they sat in silence.

Rex glanced up at her. "Much of a coffee drinker?" he asked.

"No, Sir," Kim replied. "Grew up with tea, in India."

"But you were born here."

"Yes, Sir. But I spent at least ten of my first twenty years of life bouncing back to my relatives in India. Then, some summers with my Mother's family in Argentina."

Rex kept reading her file. "By the way, knock off the 'Sir' crap," ordered the Senior Agent. "That was my Father, and I'm not in the military, neither are you."

Kim gave Rex a bit of a hard look, then asked, "Then what *do* I call you?"

Rex looked over the top of his reading glasses as he replied. "I've been called all manner of names and insults over the years. But you can call me Rex, or Agent Moyer, or even my nickname T-Rex because I am considered a dinosaur." He paused for a minute, set the file down, then continued speaking.

"Look it. I helped train Matt Swenson. Not in all that fancy Cyber Security. But just in being a good basic Agent. I especially made sure he would not get himself or others hurt or killed. Or get himself fired. I consider him a friend."

"Then why the problem I sense with training me... Rex." Kim blurted out. "I just turned thirty, so I am not what some would call a young pup straight out of college."

Rex grunted, then replied. "I realize that. And according to your file, you have some very unique skills. VERY unique." He again picked the file up, opened it, and read from it.

"*Kalaripayattu.* Indian martial arts. The Physical Training Specialist at the Academy said you kicked butt on the self-defense mats. And you received the Physical Fitness Award 'despite' being the second oldest person in your class. You also are deadly with a long gun, especially a Twelve Gauge Pump. Most women have trouble handling the recoil of shotgun slugs. But no, not you."

Rex turned a page and continued. "And you speak four languages like a native. Plus, have a scientific, forensic background." He shut the file again.

"So why, in all that is holy, do you want to start over as an entry-level Criminal Investigator?" he asked. "Especially as you come from a family with a very successful business. Yes, I know your father's company. I've done some Customs Brokers investigations where his name came up."

Rex stared at Kim, pushed for an answer. "Come on, why? You are definitely going to get your feminine hands dirty if you stick around here, around people like me."

Kim looked back at the older Agent. She saw the lines in his face, a hardness in his eyes that said he had definitely *not* been a desk jockey. So how does she tell someone like that, what she, as a not so young woman, wants?

"Okay, 'Rex,'" Kim replied. "You want an answer? Let me start by showing you something."

Out of her concealed carry purse, where she kept her back-up pistol in the sleeve pocket, she pulled a small key chain out. She handed it to Rex.

"See that odd key fob on my key?" she asked.

Rex took it, felt the furry surface, and said, "That is a large claw on the end."

"Yes, it is."

Rex frowned and asked. "Catclaw?"

Kim smiled as she replied. "Good eyes. Bengal Tiger to be exact."

Rex snorted an answer. "Keep *that* out of sight of all the PETA assholes around here. They'll throw red paint on you for having real fur. How'd you get it?"

"Helped kill it," was her short reply. Rex stared at her more. "Are you bullshiting me, Agent?" He asked in a firm tone

"I'll never kid about killing," Kim stated just as firmly. "Both my father and his brother were military types. My father got out, started the business after some skirmishes with Pakistan and the Taliban. My Uncle Abhaidev did not. Plus, he had some contacts with the state-run zoos and wildlife agencies, like our U.S. Fish and Wildlife. One day, a Bengal started killing people."

Kim still remembered it as if it were last week as she explained to the Senior Agent. She had been visiting her Uncle Abhaidev, "Abe" to his Americanized niece, while her father and mother remained in the U.S. Her uncle, though still a practicing converted Sikh and basically a vegetarian, was a crack shot in the military. He had helped hunt men, why not a tiger? So, he used his contacts to go along. And, took along his favorite niece. Kim.

"So you went on a tiger hunt with your uncle?" asked Rex.

"Yes," replied Kim. "My father threatened to beat him after he found out. My mother, with her Argentine sensibilities, threatened to gut him with a knife."

Rex let out a short, hard bark of a laugh.

"Sounds like my kind of parents!" he said. "So your uncle killed the tiger?"

Kim's eyes glazed over for a moment as the incident flashed back through her mind. Then she jerked herself back to the present and explained to her Training Agent.

"The Bengal was no normal tiger. It made it through the lines of jungle beaters, the other hunters, and began to hunt *us*. My uncle and I."

Tiger eyes flashing in the jungle brush. Then the charge, Kim never told anyone she occasionally had nightmares about it.

"What happened, Kim?" Rex's tone was now softer.

"My uncle shot her," was her reply. "It was a female. But it slammed into him, started to crush his head. So I shot it with an old Howdah pistol my uncle had me carry as back up.   Equivalent to a heavy-loaded twenty gauge."

They say silent for a moment.

"I thought Tigers were a protected species," Rex said.

"India does not like to admit it, but they don't try to capture man-eaters." She knew her reply was not P.C.

Kim looked directly into Rex's eyes as she continued.

"Since that day, I've never wanted to do anything that would be considered in most cultures as 'normal.' I want to make a difference, do meaningful work, and not be some office worker. So, after a taste at forensics, I felt law enforcement calling me."

The food came at just that moment, and they smiled at the wait staff. The Agents began to eat in silence.

Rex broke this silence.

"Kim Kupar, I wanted to coast my last year to retirement. Now, a new start-up group, a new Agent to train, shit, I can't. So. Sorry if I'm a bit pissed off. But I guess no rest for the wicked."

He looked into her eyes as he continued. "But I do not do things half-assed. I will teach you and keep you out of trouble at least until Matt comes back." He stuck his hand out across the table. "Deal?"

Kim allowed herself a small smile, took his hand, and shook it.

"Hmmm. Your Dad taught you how to shake hands, didn't he?" Asked Rex.

"Yes. And my uncle," Kim answered. "Western society today mandates a firm handshake if you are to be taken seriously. There is little bowing like in the East."

"Good. Well, let's finish stuffing our faces, then I'll show you around—"

Just then Mother Bao greeted someone with great enthusiasm. Kim, who had her back to the door as Rex had grabbed the 'overlook' seat, turned her head to see who was coming into the Jade Garden. She saw a tall, close to six-foot Chinese man, dressed in an elegant silk suit, shirt, tie and all. Kim immediately saw he had the good looks of an Asian Movie Star, and carried himself with the confidence of one.

"Wel, I'll be damned," Rex said. "One of the men you need to meet. The Gods smile on us."

Mother Bao had apparently pointed Rex out to the Chinese man as he made a beeline to their table, a smile on his face. Rex stood up to meet him.

"Agent Rex Moyer," the Chinese man said with a pleasant and robust voice. "I swear you are becoming Chinese, as you eat so much of our food." He stuck his hand out to shake the Senior Agent's hand. Kim had stood up also, turned slightly to give him a close look.

"John Wang. Ever the politician." Rex said, then loosened his hand from the other's grasp, and motioned toward Kim.

"Please meet Agent Kim Kupar. She's been on the job for about year, including training."

John turned and flashed a warm smile as he looked at Kim. As he gave her once over, Kim did the same to him. She liked what she saw, he was definitely a handsome man.

"And Rex, where have you been hiding this young lady?" The handsome man said. "In some dusty basement at the Federal Building?"

Kim beat Rex to the answer, giving a slight bow as she presented her hand to shake, then spoke in Mandarin.

"It is a pleasure to meet you. Mister Wang. I believe I've heard my father speak of you."

Wang's eyes widened a bit, then his smile turned into a grin. *"Kupar!"* He answered in kind with Mandarin. *"Of course. And you speak Mandarin like a native Chinese. You must be the daughter of Balraj Singh Kupar, a member of the Seattle Asian Business Association."*

"Yes, Sir. I believe my father has imported some electronic equipment for you."

John looked at Rex.

"How did you steal this young lady from her Father, Agent Rex?" Wang asked in English. "She is definitely much too classy for your organization."

Rex grunted and replied. "Ever the comedian, John. I believe she came to ICE Investigations as a complete volunteer."

John smiled at Kim again.

"As President of the Association, may I welcome you to the International District, traditionally known as Chinatown," John said with a bit of a regal tone. "For some reason, the term 'Chinatown' has taken on a less than respected air. Why I do not know." He looked at Rex.

"I am fascinated how Caucasians seem to decide for others what is offensive," the Chinese man opined. "We Chinese have lived here for decades, so of course it is Chinatown, a town where Chinese live."

Rex held up his hands as if in surrender before he replied. "Hey, don't drag me into Political Correctness. I irritate *that* crowd every time I open my mouth."

John and Kim both laughed, and she saw a bit of a twinkle in the Asian Businessman's eyes. Kim decided she liked him.

"Well, I will let you two finish your lunch before your duty calls," said John. "Rex, please call me when you have a chance. I may have some information on that missing container everyone is looking for."

"Hmm. Good. Will do, Mister President." Rex's reply prompted John to laugh again.

"Trying to *schmooze* me I think the term is," the Asian business leader said. "Or do you think I should run for President? I may do better in the other Washington than many, you know."

"Well, you were born here, so you could run John," Rex stated.

"Would you be my Secretary of Homeland Security, Rex?"

Rex laughed as he replied. "Hell, I've made too many enemies. Congress would never allow it."

John reached over and shook Kim's hand again. *"With that, I must leave."* He slipped into Mandarin. *"I do hope I will see you again, Miss Kupar."*

Kim smiled, almost grinned as she replied in kind. *"I hope I also do. And please call me Kim."*

"Yes, Kim. See you soon." John Wang gave her a quick wink as he left.

Rex looked at Kim as she watched the businessman leave. "Well, you two hit it off. Big time," he told Kim.

Kim blushed a bit as she replied. "I have heard my father talk about him in passing. But for some reason, I got the impression he would be older."

"And uglier, right?" This elicited a small laugh

from Kim and Rex actually tried to grin without breaking his face.

"Well, got a small laugh out of you," said Rex. "Let's finish our lunch on that note."

The two Agents sat back down and finished eating. Rex finished his lunch, sipped his tea.

"Kim, one word of advice," Rex said as he sipped his tea. "John Wang acts as if he wants to help us, has a definite pleasant demeanor. But bottom line, born here or not, he is still Chinese. Which means we, at least I, am nothing but a barbarian when compared to their culture."

Kim looked at her Training Officer as she replied. "Well, being as the Indian culture is about as old as Chinese culture, I would argue that point."

"You may be able to do that," said Rex, AKA T-Rex. "I'm seen by most Chinese as a government bureaucrat who is to be kept at arm's length."

"But you have a reputation of having contacts in the International community here in Seattle," stated Kim.

Rex replied, "Yeah, and it has taken me years. But when newer people take over positions, like John Wang being President of an important business group, I have to start re-inventing the wheel with some in this part of Seattle. Change seems to upset many in Chinatown, due to its long traditions."

"Well, judging by the way he greeted you, Rex, John Wang seems to respect you."

"Yeah," said Rex. "That and a couple of bucks will get you a Starbucks black coffee."

They finished their lunch, said goodbye to Mother Boa, and walked back to the G-ride. As they started to enter the Mustang, Rex spoke.

"By the way, word of advice from an 'Old Fart.' John Wang has a definite reputation as a Chinese Don Juan or maybe a Bill Clinton. He has cut a swath through many of the local eligible young single women, which has pissed off many of the more traditional Asians in the area. Not to mention the fathers and mothers of ladies from every ethnic background in Seattle."

"And the point you are making, Mister Old Fart?" Kim asked

Rex chuckled and said, "I ain't blind. And I am also not your Dad. But just like good looking women, handsome men have been known to use their looks and demeanor to manipulate people, especially those with positions of authority."

Kim gave him an exaggerated and fake wide-eyed look as she tried to reply in her best innocent girly voice. "Really? Who'd have thought *that*? Surely not this naïve young Indian girl!"

Rex stopped and stared for a moment. Then he began to laugh.

"I think, my young smart-alecky Agent, that you and I will get along just fine," Rex stated. "Now, warp speed, please. Back to the office. You and I need to sign off on some training categories."

"So, it's true," said Kim

"What is?" Replied Rex.

"In Homeland Security, to get crap done, you need to finish with the paperwork."

"You're learning, Kim Kupar, you're learning."

4.

Ray Painter, International Longshore, and Warehouse Union first line Steward walked quickly toward the crowd of dockworkers and local company officials. He saw that Hanjin Shipping and Yang Ming Corporation personnel were arguing between themselves as much as they were arguing with the longshoremen. Everyone seemed to be pointing at a specific large shipping container moved in preparation to being placed on a flatbed trailer for transport out of the Port Of Seattle pier. Now, everything was stopped dead.

"Hey, the Steward's here!" With that cry from one of the dockworkers, they all crowded around him as the Hanjin and Yang Ming personnel kept arguing in their common language, English.

"All right, what in the Hell I going on here?" Ray asked.

A senior Longshoreman, Danny Jones, with years of experience in Seattle spat on the ground, answered.

"Damned container has no markings on it. Can't find any manifest or any paperwork. Someone dumped it, sure as shit."

"Yeah, and now they are trying to blame it on us!" One of the younger Union members yelled from the back of the group.

Ray frowned. "Blame?" he asked. "Why? Containers get dumped by lazy truck drivers all the time."

"This one is different," Danny Jones said, as he took his hard hat off his gray hair and wiped his forehead.

"How, Danny."

"Walk over with me, Ray," was Danny's reply. "Take a whiff from one of its vents. Then you tell me."

Ray followed Danny over to the shipping container. The officials from the two companies saw the Union Steward and started to approach him.

"One minute, Gentlemen," Ray said in a loud voice. He always made sure that they knew the Union Steward did not work for them.

He followed Danny up to an air vent on the side of the container.

"Take a whiff, Boss," requested Danny

Ray put his nose and took a whiff. Then he jerked back so hard it was almost like a jump.

"Smells like old rotten death, don't it Ray?"

Ray stood for a minute. Then began to swear and yell, long and hard.

"Not again, not fricken again!"

He put to fingers to his mouth and whistled loudly. When everyone was looking at him he yelled.

"Call the Cops! And Customs! No goddamned way I'm being blamed for screwing up a crime scene! Not again!"

An official from Hanjin asked in accented English, "What do you mean, Mister Union Steward?"

Ray yelled at no one in particular. "Dead rotting flesh! And I don't think its beef."

Things began to happen fast after that.

Kim drove, with Rex riding shotgun. The new Forensic Investigation Group was barely a week old. Despite her newness with Homeland Security, Kim Kupar had been expected by John Salmon to set some forensic filed response kits for investigations that required taking tests and samples in the field.

"Your records say you have forensic and lab experience," stated the Group Supervisor. "So other than Cyber Forensics, you are responsible for setting up the field collection protocols as well as rounding up the equipment the Agents will need."

Salmon sneered a bit as he looked and spoke at Rex. "Of course, T-Rex here, as your Training Agent, will be responsible that you do it right. So, get it done. Don't screw up."

Luckily, Rex was a world-class scrounger. There were some long hours, but with a minimal budget for equipment, Kim and Rex soon had several Field Collection and Response Kits. Rex had even managed to have that stenciled on the surplus fifty caliber ammo cans and military field lockers he had used apparent magic to locate and obtain. When Kim had asked how Rex found the containers, as well as some items like gloves and basic disposable Hazmat Suits/overalls, plus some face masks. Rex had smiled before he replied.

"Ask me no questions, I will tell you know lies. I'll just say I called in some favors with some of my buddies at JBLM. They found some 'surplus' stuff for me."

Kim knew better than to ask for details. She

surmised that 'T-Rex' had contacts who 'surplus' some equipment for 'disposal' that was perfectly fine. Not precisely by Joint Base Fort Lewis-McChord regulations, so people could be called on the carpet for it. However, a needed task was accomplished.

Kim flashed her badge and credentials at the guard at the access gate and drove onto the waterfront area. Pier 46 was an enormous ship container and Conex off-loading area that looked nothing like a tradition ocean shipping pier. Humongous cranes and oversized forklifts could remove everything that came in on a container ship. Roll-on and roll-off capability meant that the old movies of stevedores using baling hooks to lift and tote were relegated to the mythic past. Everything was mechanized and computerized. As Kim drove down to where a crowd of people stood, she saw that Port Seattle Police were already on the scene. And of course, they were arguing with the longshoremen. There was no love lost between the two groups, cops, and dock workers.

"Let me do the talking, Kim," Rex said. "I know a lot these guys."

"Any women around?"

Rex grunted. "Maybe with the shipping companies," he replied. "A Port Policewoman or two, maybe a few female crane operators. But the Longshore Union on the docks is a last bastion of male dominance." He glanced at Kim. "Is that going to cause you a problem?"

Kim smiled. "Indian and Argentine culture are not noted for being examples of the 'women's movement,'" Kim said. "I may not agree with the attitudes, but I can deal with them."

"Good. Pull up over there. I see a Port of Seattle Police supervisor, I know."

In a few moments, Kim and Rex and were walking up to a uniformed officer with Sergeant's stripes on his sleeve.

"No rest for the wicked I see, Jim," Rex said as he walked up, hand extended to the tall and sandy-haired man.

"Well, I'll be damned. T-Rex, I heard you were retired!" the Port Policeman said

"Not hardly. This young Agent is Kim Kupar, my partner in training. Kim, meet Jim Reed, Port of Seattle Police Sergeant."

Kim shook his hand. "Pleased to meet you, Sir."

Jim grinned a bit and was a bit slow in releasing her hand. "Pardon me, Ma'am, but you are a lot more pleasant looking than Rex's last partners," Jim said through his grin.

Kim gave a light laugh and removed her hand from the Sergeant's grasp as she replied. "You are not the first who have said that, Sergeant Reed."

Rex broke in. "Alright, Jim, what do we have?" Jim Reed pointed to a large shipping container a few dozen yards away. All the people on the pier were giving it wide berth. "I think that is that missing container you were looking for. The one, your informant, said had a cargo of contraband."

"Why is everyone standing so far back?" asked Kim.

"Because it smells like death," said the Sergeant. "There is something dead in there, and it is not rotting fish."

"Still sealed?" Rex asked.

"Yep. There's a U.S. Customs Seal still on the door."

"Well, Jim, let us get some Hazmat suits and masks on so we don't ruin our street clothes—" Rex's comment was interrupted by another voice.

"Is that T-Rex I see?" Ray Painter called out and began to walk up to the three LEOS.

"Yes, it is," replied Rex. "How are you, Ray?"

"Hell, I thought you had retired down near Mexico!" Ray continued.

"Not hardly." The two men shook hands, Kim noticed there was tension between the Steward and the Port of Seattle Police Sergeant. But not between Rex and this man.

"Ray, want you to meet a new Agent. Kim Kupar," Rex said as he motioned towards Kim. "She is a bit of a science whiz."

Ray smiled at Kim as he gave her the old once over, 'breasts to butt.' Kim ignored him.

"Well, you're not put together like most of the other Cops around here," opined the Union Representative. "So, did T-Rex tell you that he and I did a tour in the Sand Box together?"

"Not yet, Mister Painter," Kim replied.

"Ray here is the Longshore Union Steward," interjected Rex. "He can be a pain in butt. However, we have an understanding."

"Nothing like getting shot at to make people Buds. Served in the military, Lady?" Ray asked.

"No, Sir."

"Well, our loss," Ray said, as he looked at Rex. "You going to put those white suits on?"

"Yep. The smell of dead bodies tends to permeate

and ruin street clothes."

"Well, that container sure stinks," said Ray.

Sergeant Reed broke in. "So, can you tell me who brought that can in, Painter?"

"Hell, do I look like a Teamster?" Ray replied with an edge in his voice.

"They bring them in, you guys stack 'em up," Jim Reed shot back.

"Ask the gate guard!" snapped Ray. "Bet you they were asleep last night when no crews were working."

"Sure. See no evil, hear no—" the Port Policeman continued the argument,

Kim could tell this was a continual argument between the Port Police and the Longshoremen. She knew that the Port Police arrested Longshoremen for theft when they could catch them, and some of the dock workers had criminal histories as the ILWU was not picky if you had a strong back. However, Kim knew this dispute would get everyone nowhere. So she broke into the argument.

"Gentlemen. Can we forego this conversation until I can look inside? I may find something that will help determine where this container came from, and when."

The Steward and the Sergeant both looked at her.

"She has a point, Guys," Rex stated.

Ray smiled and made a sweeping gesture toward the container. "After you, Milady," he said using his best theatrical voice.

Sergeant Reed grunted and stepped back.

Kim and Rex finished putting on their Hazmat suits. Before they put on their breathing masks, Kim took a series of digital photographs of the container, with some close ups of the metal Customs Seal. Then Rex cut the seal and swung open the large metal door. Kim stepped in with a high powered flashlight and saw the immediate cause of the reported stench. Two human bodies lay near the front, with another object in a cage toward the rear. Kim walked with a careful stride to the cage and shown her light on the contents.

"Dead adult Panda Bear, Rex," said Kim.

"You're kidding me, right?" Rex's mask-muffled voice asked.

"Wished I were. Two dead young women, it looks like, and a Panda Bear. Why would they be smuggled together?" Kim asked.

Kim walked slow, looking around the interior of the container.

"This was not the original transport container," commented Kim. "The two female bodies and the bear were taken from somewhere else and dumped in this one. Whoever did this understands police forensics capabilities."

Kim took photos of the entire interior, looking for anything that would shed light on the why and how. There was nothing.

"Rex, someone wiped this container clean before putting the bodies in here," Kim stated. "Why?" replied Rex. "Why take the chance of someone seeing this can being dumped here? Hell, I'd just dump the bodies in Puget Sound."

Kim shook her head 'no' as she answered. "If you did that, someone may have found them within twenty-four hours. These bodies have been here for some time as they are bloated and rotting. Maybe at least four days. But that is a rough estimate. We will need a full Coroners exam to find a more accurate time of death."

Rex swore, then continued. "Come on. Nothing that the Port and Seattle Police can't do."

They stepped out of the container and shut the door, then peeled off their masks.

"I bet those women are Asian. Some Snakehead dumped them here, along with that smuggled Panda," Kim said. "I'll call the Woodland Park Zoo, and Fish and Wildlife. They may be able to help me track the origin of that bear."

"Panda's come from China. What's the mystery, Kim?" asked the Senior Agent.

"It may not be wild," replied Kim. "The Chinese are breeding captive exotic and endangered animal species for private sale. That is in direct violation of international protocols."

Jim and Ray walked up to the two Agents.

"Well," asked the Union Steward. "Dead body stink, right?"

"Yes, Sir," Kim answered as she unzipped her Hazmat suit, and Rex helped her take it off.

"Human and a bear. All dead a few days at least."

Kim helped Rex take off his Hazmat suit as the Port Police Sergeant looked at Ray.

"So I ask again, Painter," said Jim. "How did this can get here, then stacked with these others, with no one seeing it until now?"

"And I say, Reed, ask the security guards!" the Union Steward heatedly replied. "Or one of the shipping companies. My crew has not been working nights."

Kim stopped the two men from continuing their long term dispute by busting into the argument.

"It is true that the container could have been moved last night, after sitting off-site for some time?"

She asked. There were nods 'yes' as the two men glared at each other

She looked at Painter, then spoke. "But I would like to talk to you men. Maybe someone saw something or someone... strange, out of place. That did not register until now."

Painter frowned. "You're not going to start accusing them of anything, are you?" He asked. "As the Steward, I can't allow that."

"Come on, Ray," Rex jumped in. "No bullshit. We are just trying to find out how two women wound up being dead, here, in the can."

The Steward looked at Rex. "If it were anyone else asking—" he began to comment.

"Yeah, Yeah," Rex butted in. "Now, how about letting us talk to them?"

"Oh all right, you old pain in the ass," Ray Painter replied. He whistled and motioned his people over.

"I'll call SPD and our people," Sergeant Reed interjected. "They can get some more forensics and the Coroner down here." The policeman purposefully stepped back, as he knew his presence would just make the Longshoreman more on edge.

A dozen suspicious dockworkers formed a half circle around their Union Steward and the two Special Agents as Ray spoke.

"Alright, Guys. Listen up. All T-Rex and... Agent Kupar want to do is ask a few questions about the can—"

"Why should I talk to some raghead woman?" a tall and slender male yelled out. He looked maybe eighteen years old if he were lucky. Ray glared at him.

"Look it, Joey. Don't be an ass," Ray shot back.

"Ass?" the youth continued. "She looks like those sonsabitches who blew my brother's leg off in Raghead Land."

Kim noticed Rex stepped off to the side a bit. She now knew that this was becoming a test of how she handled herself in the field. Well. So be it. She stepped forward to speak.

"I am part Punjabi and part Argentine, not Afghani nor Iraqi. So, you have no fight—"

Joey stepped forward, face flushed with anger. "Why don't you just take your smelly ass back to your piece of shit sand hut and—"

As he spoke, Joey reached out with his right hand to either shove or grab her shirt front. All he achieved was a light touch near her left breast. Kim's right hand was a blur as she delivered a hard open hand slap to the offending dockworkers left ear. As Joey staggered and started to yelp in pain, Kim trapped his right hand into a painful wrist lock, then swept his feet out from underneath him with a hard leg sweep. The young and stupid man slammed down hard on the pier surface. Kim put her foot on his throat.

"Where I come from, you don't lay hands on women unless asked," stated Kim

Two older Longshoreman moved to Joey's defense, spoke loudly.

"Hey, Bitch…"

Kim had her collapsible baton out, in a Short Stick Stance. She heard and felt Rex next to her

"Back off!" Rex growled. "Unless you want to lose some teeth, and spend time in the federal lock-up." To punctuate the last, he deployed his baton with a hard flick of his arm.

Everyone seemed to freeze for a moment. Then Ray Painter began to laugh.

"Damn, T-Rex!" he said in a loud voice. "Is she related to you? She seems as hard-ass as you."

The Steward stepped over the laid out Joey.

"Would you mind letting him go, Agent?" he asked.

"Okay." Kim released the man's hand and took her foot off his neck. Joey started to roll to his feet.

"You effing pig—" Joey began to say, and Ray Painter stomped his large foot down on Joey's chest.

"Stay down, dammit," the Union Steward commanded. "Before your mouth writes a check your ass can't cash."

The Steward looked at the men, used a loud and firm voice. "T-Rex and the young lady just need to ask a few questions, see if you guys saw or noticed anything strange or different the last few days. That's it! Got it?"

"Got it, Boss," Danny Jones answered. With the Senior Man going along, the rest acquiesced with a bit of grumbling.

Ten minutes later, the Longshore crew walked off for a smoke and chew break. Rex looked at Kim.

"Well, we tried."

"Yes, we did," replied Kim. "When the Coroner and the rest get here and move the bodies, I'll try to get some fingerprints, if the hands aren't too screwed up."

Rex actually shivered as he spoke. "Ommph. Taking prints off a bloated corpse? I'll let you have the pleasure."

Kim laughed as representatives from Hanjin and Yang Ming walked up. They gave short bows, and the man from Yang Ming spoke in English.

"Pardons, Agents. But have you found out where the container came from?"

Kim answered in Mandarin, which caused the Taiwanese man's eyes to widen. *"No. Sir. I am sorry. And I am sorry to say that there are two Asian women's bodies in there. So, we will have to have a look at all your recent manifests, see if we can find a connection with one of your shipments and this strange container."*

In Taiwanese-accented Mandarin, the official agreed. Then the Korean official from Hanjin spoke in accented Mandarin. *"We will provide all that you ask, Customs Officer. We would also would like any information as to where the bodies may come from. A family or two are missing daughters."*

Kim thanked them both, exchanged business cards with them, and with traditional Asian cultural respect said goodbye.

As she and Rex left the area, Rex chuckled.

"You learn fast, Agent Kupar," he said. "Letting that dockworker off with just some bruises gained you respect with a rough bunch of guys."

Kim shrugged a bit as they walked toward her G-Ride.

"Why beat someone down more than necessary?" she answered. "They did try to help us."

"Yes, and I can tell the Hanjin, and Yang Ming officials showed you some respect also," Rex said.

Kin frowned as she spoke. "As soon as the Coroner and the other forensic people from the Port and SPD are done, I'll get those fingerprints from the bodies, run them through our IDENT and the AFIS system. I doubt that they ever entered the U.S. before, legally or not. But the families need to know what happened to a young woman that was someone's daughter. They will want to arrange a burial if possible."

"And if we can't find out who they are, Kim?" asked the Senior Agent.

She paused, then looked at Rex as she spoke. "If you asked Mr. Wang to help with burial arrangements...?"

Rex laughed, then replied. "You ask. Judging by the looks he gave you the other day, I think he will do almost anything if you accepted a lunch or dinner date."

"That would be—" Kim began to say.

"Kim, that would be okay," Rex stated. "Is he under investigation? Not that I know of. Until we think he is up to no good, having a little fun with someone in the local community is allowed."

T-Rex gave her a sly smile as he continued. "You do know how to have fun, right?"

Kim blushed a bit. "You are beginning to sound like my Mother," Kim said. "Always pushing me to go out, make new friends."

"Sounds like my type of woman," Rex commented.

"Well, you don't want me to have grandchildren, do you?" the female Agent asked. "That's what she wants. Settle down with a husband from a good family, then me barefoot and pregnant."

Rex began to laugh.

"What is so funny, Senior Agent Moyer?" Kim asked.

"The thought of you being barefoot and pregnant," her Training Agent replied. "Even in this short time, I know you would not be content to be someone's stay at home wife."

Kim harrumphed. "Now you sound like my Father," she said.

"Like I said, they sound like my type of parents," opined Rex.

Any further conversation on the subject was cut short by the arrival of the Coroner.

"Start looking for the Roach Coach coffee truck, Kim. This is going to be a long day."

Kim soon realized this was a vast understatement.

5.

Kim Kupar spent a late night at Pier 46, then was back in the office on Second Avenue in Seattle early in the morning. She had managed to obtain some decent finger and toe prints from the two human corpses and was now looking for marches in IDENT and AFIS. So far, No Joy. Kim knew the chances of any of the prints showing up in either computer record system were remote. The two women were probably just barely out of their teens, so the trip they had made to get to the United States was their first. And now, it was their last.

Kim also reviewed the initial information on the Giant Panda Bear. As she had surmised, there were indications of it being bred in captivity. Further tests completed by zoologists and veterinarians would find signs of genetic modifications if her suspicions were correct. As she reviewed the sparse evidence seized at the Pier, she heard a familiar voice.

"You going to check that stuff in today, Agent Kupar?" A male voice asked. "Quicker you do it, the shorter and better the chain of custody."

Kim looked up and smiled at Alan White, the Evidence Technician assigned to SAC Seattle. A light-haired man with a receding hairline, he had a reputation for being very anal in his duties, which irritated most of the other Agents. But Kim, with her laboratory background, understood the need for accuracy and organization. Thus, she made allowances for his sometimes irritating manners. "Hi, Alan," she replied. "I see you are here early, too."

Alan looked at the items she had in evidence bags as he answered.

"I like to be here before everyone else shows up. Gives me more quiet time, less loud, and pain in the butt Agents to complain and bother me." He glanced at her and saw her smile.

"I don't mean you. You understand the reason behind procedures. Doing things the right way all the time, no short cuts."

Kim chuckled as she spoke. "I know you don't mean me, Alan. My lab experience taught me the importance of the 'Scientific Method,' as if you don't pay attention to detail, you wind up with a busted experiment or contaminated samples. Then you have to start all over again."

Another voice broke in. "Here's a coffee, Alan. Tea for you, Kim." Rex handed Alan his coffee, offered Kim her tea.

"What are you doing here so early?" Kim asked.

"You forget, young Agent, you are still technically in training status," 'T-Rex replied. "So, I have to make sure you are not out running around or bothering our Evidence Technician Extraordinaire here—"

"She's no bother, T-Rex," Alan said. "Unlike some hard-headed older Special Agents, I know."

Rex laughed at Alan's remark. He also had a good working relationship with Alan, as he had been around long enough to know what happens when evidence is screwed up, and a prosecution is lost.

"See if I bring you any more coffee," stated Rex. "So, Kim, any more pieces put together?"

Kim pointed at the computer screen as she explained. "Still no fingerprint records in any of the databases for the two unknown dead women. So, they will probably remain Jane Does unless someone comes looking for them."

"Goddamn asshole Snakeheads. Pardon my French," commented the Senior Agent

"I've heard worse, Rex," Kim replied. "I also agree with your assessment. Anyone who deals in Human Trafficking, especially young women for sex, has a special place in Hell waiting for them."

Kim picked up a couple of about to be sealed evidence bags. "However, I took samples of their clothing, also found some Chinese clothing tags," she explained. "Those items should help us track them back to at least the general point of origin in China. I doubt that the Snakeheads would spend the extra cost to give them fresh clothes of American origin."

"So they are Chinese?" Alan asked.

Kim sighed. "As well as I can tell. Bloating and rot does not help in identification of racial groups. At least, until we can get a DNA workup."

Alan shook his head. "Glad I am not expected to

take samples from corpses," commented Alan. "Marijuana samples are smelly enough."

"Well, Alan, I guess it will come with the territory of this new Group," replied Kim. "At least for members like me."

At that time a scowling John Salmon stuck his head into the small room used for evidence processing,

"Well, what happened," he demanded.

"Nice day at the shore," Rex quipped. "Salt sea breeze, and the stench of rotting bodies."

Salmon glared at him, then turned his attention to Kim. "If you can't find out who these women were in the next couple of days, close the case," he commanded. "There will be others involving live subjects to work on."

"Sir, a little effort now and we may find out if we have a Snakehead cell targeting—" Kim tried to explain.

"I said, close it out. I don't need my female Agents running all over the place." He glared at Rex again, snapped at him. "I expect you to keep her under control, Senior Agent Moyer."

"Welded and joined at the hip," Rex said in a loud voice. "Why, I even followed her into the Ladies Room until the other Agents complained."

Alan laughed at this, which drew another scowl from Salmon. "Just do it," he snapped, then stormed off.

Kim looked at Rex, and asked, "Has he always been so impatient? And so, joyful?"

Rex laughed. "He is the epitome of the Peter Principle," Rex explained. "Promoted to the level of his incompetence. So he's stressed out all the time." "And he is going to D.C," interjected Alan.

Rex snorted, then continued. "Their loss, our gain.

Kim, let me know when you are done with processing what you collected. Then—"

The intercom connection on the office telephone clicked on. "Rex, are you back there?" The soft voice of the Administrative Assistance Bettie came out of the speaker.

"Here, Bets. Whatcha need?"

"You have a Mr. Wang in the foyer,' Bettie said. "He would like to speak with you."

"Be right there." Rex looked at Alan. "Hey, could you—" he began to ask.

"Sit on these few evidence bags before they are officially turned over to me? For Agent Kupar, yes," said Alan.

Rex chuckled again, then spoke. "I guess coffee bribes are a waste of money. Come on, Kim. John Wang may be asking for me, but I know he would prefer to see you."

"Now. Rex—" began Kim.

"Come on," Rex said. "Times a wasting. Thanks, Alan."

John was dressed in a dark high-end three-piece suit with a color-coordinated silk shirt and tie. When he saw Kim with Rex, his face lit up, and his mouth broke into a sparkling smile.

"Agent Kupar! What a pleasant surprise," he said in flawless English.

"See Kim. I told you he likes you better than me," interjected Rex.

Kim tried not to blush, smiled, and put her hand out to shake. John took it in a firm handshake, then lightly added his other hand. His smile disappeared, replaced with a serious look as he spoke.

"I understand in some reports from the Asian shipping companies, you were forced to deal with the remains of a couple of my deceased countrywomen. I'm sorry you were drug into such unpleasant matters."

Kim shrugged answered as she enjoyed his touch. "Part of my job, Mr. Wang."

"Please. It's John. And death is never pleasant." His voice sounded warm and caring.

"She handles it like a trooper, John," Rex added.

John Wang looked at Rex. "I can imagine she does," John said. "But it is not something I would want a young lady to have to deal with."

Slow so as not to offend, Kim removed her hand from John's grasp, still enjoying the contact of her skin with his.

"I appreciate your concern, John," she replied. "But as the saying goes, it comes with the job."

John smiled at her again. In Mandarin, he spoke. *"As they say in the ancient Chinese Curse, may you live in interesting times."*

"I would have it no other way, John Wang," Kim replied in Mandarin. *"I want to live a full and productive life."*

"Productive... in all ways human?" John continued.

Kim looked into his eyes and felt a spark that she had not felt in a long while.

She then mentally shook herself, reminded herself she was at work.

"Possibly. Given the right circumstances. But I now have a question of you."

"Please. Ask away," the businessman answered.

"If we cannot find the identities of two deceased

Chines women, can you assist me in obtaining funeral services in the Asian community?" Kim asked. *"I know I am being forward—"*

John grinned as he answered. *"Done and done!"* He then turned toward Rex, who for once was not complaining about being left out of a conversation in Chinese.

"My friend T-Rex," John said in English. "Be very careful. I may try and hire, or steal, this young lady away from you. She has a caring heart under a very professional demeanor."

Rex lightly laughed, then answered. "I'm not worried. But it would be her decision either way. Though 'stealing' her may be a problem if she resisted."

"That is true," commented John Wang. "Already the dockworkers talk about the East Indian woman who you dare not call a 'raghead.'"

"Actually, John, it was when a certain idiot decided to lay hands on her," explained Rex. "That will not be attempted again anytime soon."

John widened his eyes in fake surprise. "Perish the thought!" he exclaimed.

Kim tried not to giggle like a school girl. Talking with John Wang made her feel years younger. However, she must force herself to concentrate on the task at hand.

"One more request, Sir," said Kim. "Since I can tell you have many contacts in the Greater Seattle area, I would appreciate any help you can obtain in discovering anything you may know of similar women. I imagine that there have been many smuggled in by sex trafficking Snakeheads over the years.

John Wang frowned, then answered. "Yes.

80   JADE EYES

Unfortunately, when I took over as the President of our business association, I soon discovered many in the Asian community have adopted the traditional Asian 'Code of Silence' when it comes to dealing with crimes and criminals in our community. Police Officials are traditionally looked on with distrust."

He lightly patted Rex's shoulder as he continued. "But I have already promised my new good friend here, T-Rex as you call him, cooperation is all such matters. And now, with pleasure, I promise the same with you, Kim."

Kim responded with a broad smile. "I look forward to working with you, John," she said.

John presented a similar broad smile. "And I you, Kim," he replied. "Now, if I may so bold as to ask what you're planning o do for lunch—"

Rex broke in. "She has some evidence processing to complete, basic reports to write. No rest for the wicked."

"I'll call you," Kim blurted out before she realized what she had said. Her traditional Argentine Mother would be scandalized that she was being so forward. Yet at the same time, she was always pushing for Kim to be with 'a nice young man.'

"Excellent!" John exclaimed. " I will wait for the cellphone call with joyous expectation."

Had anyone else used that expression, Kim would have rolled her eyes at someone spouting bovine excrement. With John Wang, it seemed real, genuine... and welcomed on her part.

The Agents escorted John to the elevator and said their goodbyes. Rex and Kim walked back to the evidence area, Rex gave her a sly smile as he spoke.

"Just remember what I said about John Wang. He is the commensurate politician, which means he can B.S. with the best of them when he wants some inside information. Or when he sees a pretty lady."

Kim smiled back as she replied. "You forget I am not some college girl, just graduated. I've dealt with many John Wangs while working with my family's business, then in the science laboratory world."

"Okay. Just don't say I didn't warn you," said Rex.

"*Yes, Respected Elder,*" she answered in Chinese.

"What?" Responded Rex

"I said yes, of course."

"Okay. Back to work."

It was Noon when Kim escorted Alan down the couple of blocks to the old Customs House and Federal Building where the combined Evidence Vault for ICE and Customs and Border Protection (CBP) seizures and investigations resided. Alan asked Kim to help escort him as, in addition to her case evidence, he had some drug samples, plus some seized currency in his extensive backpack. All needed to be 'put to bed.'

"If something ever turns up missing, I don't want to be the one who was left alone, holding the bag," Alan had explained to Kim. The Instructors at the ICE/HSI Academy had warned her and her classmates many times about how not to draw the attention of Internal Affairs, known as the Office of Professional Responsibility in Homeland Security. Always having someone to witness any evidence handling, especially currency, was a key element to keeping out of trouble.

Kim had met the Senior Customs and Border Protection (CBP) Evidence Technician, Kregg Sorenson, when she had first reported into the Seattle Office. He was a former Army Vet who was a close friend of Rex, as well as a Uniformed Officer who had impressed Kim with his organizational abilities connected with a pleasant demeanor. Alan had also told her that Kregg helped keep Agents who listened to him out of trouble with evidence procedures. She and Alan rounded the corner onto the lower street where the back of the old Customs House faced. The Evidence Room and Vault was near the rear loading dock. There were still some subordinate offices and storage rooms in this historical U.S. Federal Building, so it was even used daily by other agencies.

Coming toward the two ICE personnel were three women wearing full Muslim *burqas* where only the eyes could be seen. Kim had seen many such examples of restrictive Muslim Dress in her travels on the part of her family's business. However, something seemed to be off in this instance.

"Where is the male family member?" Kim mumbled to herself as the two groups began to pass each other.

"What?" Alan said, thinking Kim had spoken to him. Then all Hell broke loose.

One of the 'women' slammed into Alan, knocked him into the stone side of the former Customs House. One of the others grabbed at Kim, with the third going for Alan's backpack. Kim used a broad arm sweep to break the attempt to grab her, followed up with a robust front kick to the stomach of the Burqa wearing figure. She went for her pistol.

Arms wrapped her from behind as someone rattled off Mandarin near her ears. The figure which grabbed her from behind was dressed in Western street clothes and yelled at the other three to hurry up and get the pack from Alan. But the Evidence Tech was having none of that. He yanked his pistol out as he began to curse loud and long. One of the figures grabbed the pistol hand and used a nasty hand and wrist technique to tear the pistol loose and send it into the street. Alan head-butted the one figure trying to wrap his/her arms around him. The Evidence Tech had grown up on the rough streets near Detroit and was not a stranger to the rough and tumble. The head-butted figure stumbled back, howling in a particular male timbre. Kim stopped grabbing for her handgun, instead reached low and behind her, found the manhood of the Chinese man holding her. He screamed as she twisted and crushed. The arms wrapped around her let go, the Chinese man dropped to his knees in excruciating pain. The figure she had kicked came at her with a blade.

Hours of *Kalaripayattu* training set Kim into a knife and bladed weapon defense. Hard open-handed slaps knocked the knife away and to the side, opening up the body of the Burqa wearing figure to a fast and hard high kick to the nose and eye area. As the person stumbled back, Kim took the now identified male's legs out with a solid leg sweep, dumping him on the hard sidewalk. Alan yanked out his handheld radio and keyed the mike.

"Officer—!" The figure that had yanked his pistol from him now grabbed at his radio. Alan cursed loud and punched at the attacker, the two falling to the street in a tumble. Kim stepped toward Alan, and the head butted figure grabbed at her. A twist and he was sent flying with an Indian variation of a hip throw. Kim saw motion to her side, looked to see Mister Crushed Manhood pointing a pistol at her. As time slowed, she knew she could not draw her own sidearm before she was shot.

The Chinese man's head exploded in a red mist as Kim's ears rang from the echoing gunshot. She instinctively ducked, then looked at the gunshot's source. Standing at the corner with a Glock pistol in his hand was John Wang. The figure she had thrown to the street jumped to his feet and began to run as fast as a Burqa would allow. The second figure followed. In a split second, Kim decided to jump to Alan's aid rather than chase the two runners. As she dashed up to the struggling figures, Alan began to beat the man's head in with his radio.

"You no good fucking piece of dogshit!" Alan bellowed as he beat the man senseless.

"Alan! Stop! We need to be able to question him."

Alan looked at Kim, slammed the attackers head down onto the hard sidewalk, and then stood up.

"*Nobody* steals evidence from, Alan White!" he yelled. "Nobody!"

With long strides, John Wang was next to Kim.

"Are you okay?" he asked.

Kim looked into his eyes as she replied. "Thanks to you, yes."

"Drop the gun, Son. You okay, Alan?" It was Kregg Sorenson, the CBP Evidence Technician, standing at the Evidence Storage Area entry door with pistol in hand.

"It's okay, Officer Sorenson," Kim called out. "Mr. Wang is on our side."

"I will put my pistol down anyways, Kim," John said. "Less chance of misunderstandings."

Then, the sky seemed to open and rain Cops, badge and gun carriers of every type imaginable, on to the streets of Seattle.

An hour later and things were still being sorted out. Seattle Police Department claimed jurisdiction over the shooting until someone pointed out the Old Customs Building may still be Exclusive Jurisdiction. The dead Chinese male had fallen on the edge of the loading dock, leading to confusion. DHS/ICE Office of Professional Responsibility showed up and began to argue with the FBI, who claimed jurisdiction as it was an Assault on a Federal Officer, their area of authority. Deputy SAC Brad Ball showed up with Rex, Salmon, and Tim Weiss.

"You okay, Agent Kupar?" Brad asked.

"Thanks to Mr. Wang, yes," Kim replied.

"I thought I told you to keep an eye on her, Moyer," Salmon snapped.

"She was helping Alan transport the evidence from her case to the main vault. That is normal—" Rex began to answer.

Dave Salmon cut in. "I need some wet behind female Agent wandering around by herself like a need a hole in the head." He glared at Kupar. "How did these a-holes grab you and White? Not paying attention, worried about your makeup or something?"

Rex blushed red, started to advance on Salmon with blood in his eye. "She kicked two punk's asses. Want to be next?" Rex's question had steel in it.

"Stand down!" ASAC Weiss barked. "Salmon, watch your comments. She's a female Agent. Get over it."

"T-Rex. I don't think she needs you to jump to her defense."

"Hell, Tim. She's my Trainee…"

"Who handled a sticky situation like a pro," Weiss

cut him off.

"She almost got herself shot!" Salmon blurted out.

"Goes with the territory, Dave, You know that. She's still with us. That Chinese guy in the street isn't."

"Dammit, if not for that Wang character..." Weiss rolled his eyes skyward. "Why Me, Lord? Why Me?" The ASAC asked to the heavens. He stepped up to Salmon, ordered, "Go back to the office. Call Sector Communications, tell them what happened. Then prepare a briefing for D.C."

"I need—"

"You 'need' to get moving. You have enough info for a basic SITREP. Now, move!"

Salmon glared at Kim, who met the look. No way would she let this person stare he down. Salmon turned and stomped off.

Brad walked up to Kim. "Alan says you're a regular Bruce Lee," the DSAC commented.

"Indian, Boss," Rex interjected. "Lee was Chinese."

Brad looked at T-Rex. "No kidding," he said in a sharp tone. "Gee, I never would have noticed if you hadn't just opened your yap."

Rex looked away. "Sorry, Boss," he said.

Brad took a deep breath, let it out before he spoke again.

"Okay. We're all stressed out right now. Blood in the streets, someone attacking two of our people, are definitely not normal situations for SAC Seattle. Agent Kupar, get your evidence turned over to Mr. Sorenson there. Then hit the office, start writing up a Report of Investigation on what happened. You didn't shoot anyone, so no need to put you on Admin Leave, take your gun."

"Yes, Sir," Kim replied.

"Now, I'm going to see if the Paramedics are through with Alan. You weren't injured, Kim?" "No. Sir. Just grabbed."

"T-Rex."

"Sir."

"Make sure Mister Wang is treated right," directed the DSAC. "ICE owes him big time."

"Yes, Sir."

Brad patted Kim on her arm as he spoke. "You did good. Remember that." He nodded at Rex and walked away.

Rex stepped closer to Kim. "Not to sound like an old woman—" he began to say.

"I'm fine," Kim answered the unfinished question. "The adrenaline rush has lessened. And, as you would say, T-Rex, this is not my first rodeo. At least not in facing death."

Rex grinned. "That's right, Tiger Lady," he said.

He looked over at John Wang, who was still semi-surrounded by representatives from various law enforcement agencies, all peppering him with questions. Which he fielded with a hint of a smile on his lips, as if being questioned about a shoot-out happened every day.

"Come on," commented Rex. "Let's remind those people that John is a 'good guy' who saved your ass, not a suspect."

As Kim and Rex walked toward John, a new figure in a high priced three-piece suit strode up with an air of authority. In a commanding voice, the black haired younger man inserted himself into the conversation.

"Gentlemen. Dave Keegan of Ashcroft and Associates. Mister Wang is my client, so the interviews stop now."

Rex laughed and said. "The Calvary just arrived."

Kim gave him a quizzical look. "Who?" she asked

"Dave Keegan, lawyer extraordinaire, is an ex-ICE, Homeland Security Agent, former Border Patrol who 'saw the light' and got a law degree," Rex replied. "If he is on your side, no one screws with you," Rex called out to the well-dressed man.

"Hey, what're doing out of your office? Slumming?"

Dave looked up at the voice and grinned as he replied.

"Why did I just know you would be here, T-Rex?"

"Because I was always in the shit when you were in the ICE Investigations office," said the Senior Agent.

Dave Keegan laughed as the other law enforcement types near John stood around watching the interruption. When they all tried to jump in at once, Dave quickly re-asserted his authority.

"As I said, Ladies and Gentlemen, Mr. Wang is my client. Any further questioning can be completed later after I have had a chance to confer with him, and he has had an opportunity to decompress. He is not used to being involved in gunplay on the streets of Seattle."

A young man with a FBI badge on a chain around his neck broke in.

"Look it, we are not through questioning him..."

"Is he under arrest?" Asked Dave.

"No, but we need to take him to the office—"

"Well, unless you plan on arresting him, he isn't going. Taking him against his will to an office, he has no desire to go to is a form of arrest. This isn't television."

The FBI Agent's face began to flush. Rex chuckled.

"Quit while you're ahead, young man," Rex said. "Drag Mr. Wang to the office and all you'll get is silence and a pissed off Asian Community."

"And," added Dave Keegan, "a complaint for False Arrest. He *saved* a Federal Agent from being shot! Explain why you are arresting him after he performed that deed."

Soon all the assembled Agents and Investigators who wanted a piece of John stood around grumbling, then handed his lawyer, Dave, their business cards. Dave flashed a broad grin, then spoke.

"Gentlemen, and Lady, I will take all these nice business cards, have my staff array them in alphabetical order and set up interviews with my client. After he decompresses like I stated. You all have a nice day."

All the law enforcement officers walked away, mumbling, and were soon trying to find other persons to question, argue over pieces of evidence. John laughed loud.

"I have not seen that many disappointed faces in years!" The Asian businessman said. "Dave, my good lawyer, you made my day."

"That's why you have me on a hefty retainer." Dave looked at Kim as he spoke. "You must be the young Agent John was defending."

Kim presented a slight smile, stuck her hand out to shake. "Special Agent Kim Kupar, Sir," she replied. "If you need a statement from me—"

"I'll let T-Rex here set that up. From experience, you have a Hell of a task in front of you writing all the reports this is going to generate."

"Yes, she will," interjected Rex. "And I get to make sure it all gets done until Matt Swenson comes back from maternity leave."

"His wife had the child?" Asked Dave.

"Yes, premature. So he had to take off early. They almost lost her."

Dave Keegan frowned. "Let me know if they need anything," said Dave. "They're good people."

Rex grinned.

"I thought scum sucking lawyers associated only with other bottom feeders, not law enforcement," commented Rex. "Present company excluded."

Dave laughed.

"Same ole T-Rex." He looked at Kim, then handed her one of his cards as he again spoke. "If you ever get jammed up, call me. I take most Agents Pro Bono."

Kim smiled again. "Thank You, Sir," she replied. "Now, I must be going."

"May I walk you up the block, Agent Kupar?" John asked.

"Why, yes. Of Course," answered Kim

Rex looked at Dave Keegan and winked. "Let me bother you for a moment," the elder Agent interjected. "I have a legal question to run by you."

Dave smiled. "But of course," he responded. "Walk this way—"

John and Kim began walking up the hill toward the Second Avenue ICE Investigations Office. John gently touched her arm. "You are okay, uninjured?" he asked.

"Thanks to you, yes." Kim turned to speak to him as they walked. "I don't know how to thank you—"

"Dinner." It was a quick and sure answer in John's part.

"Dinner? I…"

"Not tonight, of course," John added. "You need to relax, decompress as friend Keegan puts it."

Kim stopped on the street, looked into John's eyes. They both smiled at the same time, as Kim lightly grasped John's hand, managed to speak without stammering.

"I will call you then. I have your card."

John used his free hand to pull out another card from a hidden inner pocket of his suit jacket.

"Private line," he said. "Call me when you can. I will be looking forward to it."

Kim felt an urge to hug him, but decided that was a bit forward, and probably unprofessional. So she flashed a broad grin. John moved a bit closer.

"Jade," he said.

"Jade? Oh, my eyes. Yes. My Mother's and Father's genes, combined somehow and I have jade eyes."

John whispered in Mandarin. *"Jade eyes reflect the temple of the soul."*

"That is not a saying I am familiar with, John ," Kim replied in kind.

"Well, I will explain its history when we meet again. My Jade Beauty."

He gently squeeze her hand as he spoke again. *"Now, shall we continue up the hill? I will make sure you reach your office, safe and sound."*

Kim laughed like she had not done for some time. It felt good.

"Of course," she replied. *"I expect no less—John."*

The day seemed a bit brighter as they continued up the hill.

6.

DOWNTOWN, SEATTLE

It was the Witching Hour when Kim reached her townhouse on First Avenue. She entered through the security entrance and went to the elevator. One excellent result from working first in the family business and then for an extensive testing laboratory was that Kim had made good money which she socked away. Thus, she had purchased this townhouse before she had decided to try for a Federal Law Enforcement Position. Luckily, her language and scientific skills, plus education resulted in her being hired on as a GS-9 as well as being able to remain in Seattle.

Her townhouse was on the third floor of the remodeled former office building from a much earlier age. The elevator was a lovely modern Otis. Kim had often mused about the possibility of an old metal cage framed lift as was still commonplace in parts of India. They had a certain Old World charm, but the Otis was definitely more reliable. The elevator transported her to her floor with a smooth and quick manner. She stepped out, her keys in her right hand, her large equipment case in her left. As she approached the door, she saw that her security system pad had been turned off. She set her case down, switched her keys to her left hand, and drew her pistol. She knew she had set the alarm and after the attack earlier in the day, anything was now possible.

She unlocked her door with as much quiet as possible, then pushed it open with a slow and smooth motion. Kim tried to emulate the quiet padding stride of a Bengal Tiger, something her uncle Abe had schooled her in. Then she heard a familiar voice singing a song in her kitchen. Her mother Guadalupe had come unannounced. Again.

Kim let out a frustrated sigh, then holstered her pistol. No use scaring her, it would not change her sometimes irritating habits. She strolled to the kitchen, announced her presence.

"Mother, if you are going sneak in, at last reset the door alarm."

Her mother Guadalupe turned around and smiled. A slender and still pretty woman with jet black hair and a lighter complexion than Kim, some had said she had the makings of a model in her younger years. On the counter was a large bouquet of various colors of roses. "Hello, my daughter," she greeted Kim. "I was just arranging and watering these beautiful flowers someone delivered. They were outside your door."

"Is there a card, Mother?" Kim asked

"Yes," replied her mother. "It is in Mandarin, which I still read with difficulty."

Kim smiled. Mother was an intelligent and educated woman but was also a bit stubborn. She learned Punjabi from her husband, spoke native

Argentine Spanish, and was fluent in English. But she resisted learning Mandarin.

"Let them learn my language for a change," she had told her husband. And that was that.

Kim took the card from her mother and read it. She could not keep from smiling, almost grinned. "Well?" Guadalupe cocked a questioning eyebrow at her daughter as she questioned her.

"It is from a friend. A John Wang."

Guadalupe furrowed her brow in concentration. "I have heard that name before," Guadalupe said.

"He is the President of the Seattle Asian Business Association," Kim explained.

With that bit of information. Guadalupe's mouth became a broad smile. "Now, I remember him!" Kim's mother said with exuberance. A fine young man, and single, I hear."

Kim sighed as she replied. "Yes, Mother. He is single."

"So how did this fortunate meeting happen, Kim?" her mother asked. Then her mother frowned again.

"This has to do with the violence this afternoon, yes? That is why I am here," Guadalupe explained. "I saw the news report, saw you walking from the scene, and heard that an East Indian Special Agent had almost—"

Kim saw a tear in Guadalupe's eye and reached over to hug her. "*I am fine, Mother,*" she said in Spanish. "*You, Father and Uncle Abe always taught me how to take care of myself.*"

"*Your uncle is the one who pushed you to be so independent!*" Guadalupe scolded. "*How could such a traditional Indian family have people who push women to act like men I will never understand."* She looked up at her taller daughter.

"Uncle Abe just wanted me to be able to protect myself, not be afraid," Kim replied. *"What is wrong with that?"*

"When it causes a fine young lady to leave home, carry weapons, arrest people, that is what is wrong," her mother lectured. *"You should have a home, your own family—"*

And Kim knew that once again, it was about marriage and grandchildren. Her older brother, Jagjit, was married to a 'nice' Indian woman and had three children already. He was the so-called right-hand man to their father in Kupar Computers and Electronics Import and Export, LTD, the eldest son who would inherit the business. Being next in line, the 'middle child' and only girl, Kim had been expected to follow tradition, marry a good man who could become part of the family business. Then, of course, Kim was to stay at home, become pregnant—

No. Not then, not now. Maybe never.

Then her younger brother by three years, Akaljot, 'A.J.' had really thrown a monkey wrench in the mix. At age nineteen, he had left home, become a bartender, and lived the life of a 'party animal.' "What will you do with your life?" Both parents had scolded him. "Working in a bar is not a career." "A career?" Akal as he was also called answered. "I want a Life!" Now her father had two rebellious children. Kim still stopped in to see her parents on a fairly regular basis. Akal did not.

Kim smiled at her mother, kissed her forehead, continues in Spanish. *"Mother, do not worry. I am fine. And I have many fellow Special Agents who will help me be safe."*

Her mother kissed her cheek, then stepped back. *"To be a mother is to worry. You will discover that when you marry and have children."*

"Mother—"

"I know, I know, don't push." Guadalupe smiled at Kim, then spoke. *"But tell me, my daughter. I understand this John Wang actually helped save you from harm. Is that true?"*

"Yes, Mother. It's true."

Guadalupe flashed a broad smile. "Now I will make some tea, and you will tell me all that you know of this fine young man," she informed her only daughter in English.

Kim sighed. A late night was about to become later. But she knew her mother would not leave until she heard the details she wanted to hear. So Kim began in Spanish. *"Okay, Mother. I and the Evidence Technician, Alan White were walking down to the evidence vault..."*

"Is he a nice young man also?" her mother asked.

"Mother, please—" It was to be a long night.

7.

ICE/HSI OFFICE, SEATTLE

Two days after her Midnight conversation with her mother, Kim was almost caught up with her paperwork. In addition to the Report of Investigation she had to write detailing all the actions on the day of the attack, she also had to field questions from some half dozen different law enforcement agencies, all asking the same questions over and over again. Then, she had called Dave Keegan to see if he still needed a statement from her.

"No, Agent Kupar," the former Special Agent replied. "I had enough from John Wang and the forensics, not to mention Alan, to show that a 'pillar of the community' came to the aid of two Federal Law Enforcement Officers who be being threatened with deadly force. In other word, they were barking up the wrong tree."

Kim smiled to herself. "Thank you, Mr. Keegan—" Kim started to say.

"Mister Keegan is my father," Dave said. "To

Agents and my friends like Rex I'm Dave. So please call me Dave."

"Then, you must call me Kim," responded Kim. "I have to ask when was it that you quit ICE and became a lawyer."

"Just five years ago," answered Dave. "That is when I went to the 'Dark Side' as T-rex likes to call it."

Kim laughed, then continued. "Well, I'm glad you did, as you kept John from being jammed up."

"Yes, I think I was successful," the lawyer agreed. "And please remember that if you ever become 'jammed,' call me day or night. Clients like John Wang pay me enough that I do pro bono for law enforcement. Now, I must bid you Adieu as I have a client waiting outside. You stay safe, Kim, and try to keep Rex out of trouble."

Kim Laughed then replied. "I will do my best. Have a nice day." She hung up her telephone and sat back for a moment. As the ancient Chinese curse John Wang had mentioned said, she was definitely living in interesting times. Possibly, they were too interesting.

The intercom on her desk phone buzzed. It was T-Rex.

"Yes S... I mean Rex," Kim answered.

"Pack up your crap. The Chinese guy Alan beat the Hell out of has recovered enough to be questioned. Come on, we'll get a jump on the FeeBees and everyone else. This has got to be connected to the Snakehead operation."

Kim frowned. "Won't that make the FBI, all the others angry?" she asked. "They still want to complete the case on the assault."

"Early bird gets the worm," said Rex. "And I do

not work for the Fan Belt Inspectors. Meet you at your car. Chop-Chop."

Kim shook her head as she hung up the phone. Chop-Chop. Did T-Rex realize he sounded like a character in an old Charlie Chan Movie?

8.

Kim pulled the Mustang into a slot not far from the Emergency Entrance. Rex was out and walking before she realized, so she had to hurry to catch up. Rex flashed his badge at the Hospital Security Officer who nodded as Rex and Kim walked by. Rex went to a bank of elevators, caught one just opening, strode in and pushed the Fifth Floor button.

"They have our friend on the fifth floor in a special room, under guard," explained Rex.

"What's his name?" Asked Kim

"Right now they have him listed under Tong," replied Rex. "He won't give us a name, played half dead."

"No records from his fingerprints?" Kim queried.

"Nope," the Senior Agent answered. "Either born here or smuggled in."

Rex looked at Kim. "Hope you can do your magic with your Mandarin," he said.

Kim smiled and replied. "I'll try."

In front of the hospital room toward the end of

the hall was a tall and bored looking Seattle Police Officer. He stood as they approached, smiled at Rex. "T-Rex. Thought you retired," the officer said.

Rex grunted. "Not yet," he replied. "Agent Kupar, please meet Corporal William Bud. I've known him for years."

Kim shook hands with the officer as she introduced herself. "Kim Kupar, Sir. Pleased to meet you."

Bud flashed a wide smile. "You're the young lady who kicked butt the other day downtown," said Bud. "Pleased to make your acquaintance."

Kim shrugged a bit. "Just doing what I had to," she said.

"Well, what you 'had' to do, made the rest of us warm and fuzzy," stated William Bud. The Corporal looked at Rex. "You want some private one on one, right?"

"Yes, Sir."

The SPD Officer produced a clipboard. "Sign here. You beat everyone," Bud said. "The FeeBees tried to say this guy was off limits. Our Chief said we have a separate case, so pound sand." Bud grinned. "After kowtowing to them because of that original Federal supervision crap, telling them to pound sand felt good."

Kim and Rex slid into the hospital room. Lying handcuffed to the bed was the Chinese man whose face had been rearranged by Alan White. The man's left eye was bandaged over, and his right was swollen, along with the rest of his face. But he still was able to recognize Kim.

"Lawyer! I want Lawyer." He cried out through his swollen lips in accented English.

"I don't think he likes you, Kim," opined Rex.

Kim harrumphed, then spoke in Mandarin. *"Go ahead. Get a lawyer. It won't do you any good. Your friends all left you, except for the one shot. If no one claims him, identifies him, he'll be buried in a paupers field."*

Something in Kim's words must have hit a nerve of 'Tong's' as he yelled back in Mandarin.

"If that son of a dog had not betrayed us, my cousin would still be alive!"

"And what son of a dog would that be?" Kim asked. The suspect realized he had said too much, clamped his mouth shut and glared at Kim with his one swollen eye. Rex laughed.

"Well, I only caught a few words of that, but did he insult someone?" Rex asked.

"He said a son of a dog betrayed him and his cousin, the dead one," replied Kim.

Rex grunted. "Well, 'Chuckles' just gave us another lead," stated Rex. "We'll have to let the Asian Community know he co-operated with us."

The injured man started to say something, then clamped his mouth tight.

"Come on Kim. We'll let the FeeBees sweat it out of him. Bye Bye now," Rex said as he gave a little wave at the man, who began to mumble under his breath as the two Agents left the room.

"Well, young lady," explained Rex, "that spontaneous exclamation may get thrown out of court due to his demanding a lawyer first, but we now know that someone else planned this. Someone that nimrod in there thinks betrayed them."

"Why?" Kim asked. "Because John Wang showed up and kept me from getting shot?"

"Who knows?" The Senior Agent answered. "There are those bad guys who are so paranoid that if something goes wrong, it must be that someone snitched on them. Like all those conspiracy theorists on late night radio. Everything happens because 'someone' screwed things up behind the scenes." He looked at Kim as they entered the elevator.

"By the way," he asked. "Does son of a dog mean son of a bitch?"

"Yes, basically," explained Kim. "Although if someone called your father a 'dog' in China, it would also be an insult."

"So Bill Clinton being a 'dog' because he couldn't keep his fly zipped—" continued Rex.

"Rosters and rabbits have more to do with phallic and fertility symbols in China than dogs," Kim replied. "Now that we have beat that horse to death—"

"Kim Kupar! I am indeed blessed today." The familiar voice of John Wang rang out as Rex and Kim exited the elevator.

Kim smiled as he approached, spoke before Rex could. "John, may I ask why you are at a hospital? Not bad news about someone you know, I hope."

John waved the statement away with a flip of his hand. "No, thank God," the Chinese businessman said. "I am here working on a new treatment center that the Seattle Asian Business Association is helping to fund. It will help deal with the elderly and needy members of our community."

"I'd swear you were stalking us, John," Rex stated. "At least you seem to be following a certain female Agent."

"Well, my friend, why would I follow a rough

looking man like you?" John replied. "Even if I were gay, I would still not find you attractive. With all due respect, of course."

Rex laughed and responded. "Insult me, then apologize. If that is not Chinese culture around here, I don't know what is."

The three then all laughed as John moved closer to Kim. He gently brushed her left hand with his fingers as he smiled and looked into her eyes. "I hope you have not been brought here by sickness," he asked.

"No, John. Just our job."

John made a show of cupping his chin in his hand, furrowing his brow in a pantomime of deep contemplation.

"Let me think—" the Chinese businessman said, then widened his eyes and exaggeratedly snapped his fingers. "I know. You came to see an injured Chinese man who had the misfortune of assaulting two Federal Agents."

Rex snorted, then responded. "I should have known that the Asian intelligence system in your community would know what is happening as quickly as we do."

The Asian Business Association President laughed.

"But of course," John said. "Next, you will be accusing me of being the typical inscrutable Asian."

Kim tried not to giggle like a little school girl. For some reason, John made her feel like she was still in high school, enjoying the days before a person had to deal with such adult subjects as crime and death. Rex noticed the change of demeanor in his young partner, smirked.

"Well, excuse me for a moment," he said. "I need to visit the little boy's room. You'll keep Kim company, right, John?"

"For my friend T-Rex, of course."

As Rex walked away, Kim leaned in a bit closer to speak.

"I haven't had a chance to really thank you. If you had not shown up when you did, I could've been—"

John waved the rest of the remark away as he spoke.

"Please. Let us not dwell on what could have gone wrong. Let us instead think about what is right." He smiled broadly at Kim.

"And what I think is 'right' at this minute, is to ask you to dinner. Would Friday night be okay?"

Kim broadly smiled as she replied. "I would like that. However, because of my work and this investigation—"

"You are afraid you will be called away, yes?" John asked. "Well, my dear, it just so happens that the dinner I'm asking you to attend is both the opening of my new restaurant and nightclub bar, 'The Jade Palace,' as well as a charity auction of Chinese art. Thus, all the 'Who's Who' of the Asian community will be there. Not to mention other local dignitaries."

John gently took her left hand in his as he continued. "You can tell the powers that be that this is an excellent opportunity for a young Special Agent to develop excellent sources of information in the sometimes closed Asian community. Especially a young and pretty lady who speaks Mandarin like a native."

Kim blushed a bit then smiled again and answered. "Then, I'll plan on attending. The dress is formal?"

"Yes," John replied. "If I may be so bold to

suggest a nice dress of East Indian style and fashion? It will help others to realize, as I have, your unique beauty."

Kim looked down, a bit embarrassed at the compliments.

"Please. I am just like many others—", Kim tried to say.

John interrupted. *"No, my jade eyed beauty,"* he said in Mandarin. *"You are far from being like many others. I look forward to having you next to me at this auspicious occasion."*

Kim look into his eyes, saw a twinkle that she knew she reflected in her own. She felt a sudden urge to kiss him. John gently squeezed her hand.

"Now, I must be off," he said. "You have the card with my private line and office address. If you ever need to contact me, just go there and show the card. My people will run to find me. Now, until Friday night."

"Yes, John. I look forward to it," Kim answered with a lilt in her voice.

John flashed one more smile, gave a short bow, and was off.

When Rex returned from his foray into the world of the hospital restrooms, he found Kim standing with a small smile and a faraway look on her face.

"Well, let me guess," the man known as T-Rex said. "Prom Date, right?"

Kim pulled herself back to reality as she replied. "You know, if you did not remind me of some Uncles I know, I'd be angry with your nosiness. But, in the spirit of the question, yes, I have a 'Prom Date.'"

Rex flashed an infrequent smile. "You know the musical 'South Pacific' by Rodgers and Hammerstein?" he asked.

"Yes. Why? "

"Well, there is a song that goes like this...' Hello young lovers, wherever you are—" Rex began to sing off key.

"You know, Rex," interrupted Kim. "At the Academy, they often used a concept that I have become very familiar with."

"And what is that, pray tell?"

"You know why they don't send donkeys to school?" The young Agent asked her Training Agent. "They don't like smartasses, Rex Moyer. "

Rex chuckled. "Oh, like I haven't heard *that* before."

9.

John Wang sent a private limousine to pick Kim up at her townhouse. During the short ride. Kim smiled at the memory of a brief meeting she had earlier in the day with Supervisor Salmon. He had stopped her in the hallway at the SAC Office.

"I have been told that no one is to bother you this weekend. Something about a request from a local dignitary," stated Salmon. The short man had frowned. "Don't get a swelled head, Newbie."

"Never. Sir," Kim replied. With that, Salmon grunted and walked off.

Kim smiled to herself. She would not let a Mister Negativity ruin this evening. Even if it had not been with John, this was the first 'date' in a long time.

She had gone to her long closet in the townhouse and looked for a unique jade vestment her Aunt Sihan had made for her.

"This will knock a man's socks off, as they say in

America," her aunt had said with a grin. It still fit like a glove in all the right places. So, when she stepped from the limousine, John's mouth dropped open a bit. He took her hand as if she were a princess and led her down an actual red carpet to the lit up main entrance of "The Jade Palace."

John finally found his voice. "Kim, you are beautiful seems bit too trite of a word. But for once, I am tongue-tied."

Kim laughed, grabbed his arm, and squeezed it. She felt his muscles underneath, and a warmth spread in her body.

"This is an Indian *Lengha*," she explained. "A skirt and top that has become popular in Indian Film." Kim stepped off to the side a bit, did a short spin around, regaling in showing off her traditional femininity, a rare occurrence for her. An ankle length silk skirt with a matching top, edged in jade gemstones, with a long silk sheer wrap that acted like a *Sari* concealing her bare midriff, but not completely. She had her hair expertly pile high, a silver necklace with a jade gemstone woven in her hair, acted like a small crown.

"I take it, Sir, you concur with my choice of evening wear?" Kim asked with glee in her voice

John stepped in close and put his arm about her waist. Kim saw a sparkle in his eyes that she knew was reflected by her own. In a move that surprised herself, Kim pulled John farther off the red carpet and into the shadows. There, she kissed him. John kissed back with a desire that matched her own. They slowly and with reluctance parted.

John whispered. "I have something for you, my jade beauty."

"You will spoil me," Kim replied. "First, you save my life. Then, you give me gifts."

He gazed into her eyes as he said: "I only give you what you deserve."

John pulled a small box from his pocket and opened it. Kim looked in a gasped. Inside was a bracelet made of the most exquisite jade.

"This will now match your *lengha* perfectly," John said.

"Please, John. This is too expensive. I cannot—" Kim tried to protest.

"Yes, you can." John was firm in his statement. "If you refuse, I'll have to throw it out. For to re-gift, it would bring bad luck."

Kim looked at John with a touch of horror in her face. "You wouldn't!" The young Agent exclaimed.

"Yes, I would. Here—" said John as he motioned as if to toss it.

Kim snatched it from him, then blushed at her action.

"I seem greedy—" she began to say.

John kissed her hand. "You are far from greedy," disagreed the handsome Chinese man. "You are a giver. I can sense it."

With that, she allowed John to put the bracelet on her left wrist. She examined it on her wrist, felt a tear develop in her eye. She started to blink it away, and John handed her a silk handkerchief.

"Here," John said. "Save your makeup. Though your natural beauty needs no enhancements."

She dabbed her eye, started to hand it back, and instead planted a quick kiss on John.

"You hardly know me, John," Kim said. "Yet you

treat me as if you have known me for years."

"We are kindred souls, my dear," explained John. "I sense it." He wrapped her left hand around his arm. "Now, as host, I must mingle. And you shall mingle with me as my special guest. With this, you will meet many local people who may help you in your investigations."

Kim looked into his face. "What do you get from this?" she asked.

John smiled as he replied. "The utmost pleasure of your company. Now, come. We circulate."

The rest of the evening seemed like a fairy tale to Kim. She soon saw that The Jade Palace was to be more of a Night Club than a small restaurant and bar. As John mingled and introduced her to everyone under the Sun, or Moon since it was nighttime, he explained his vision.

"I Plan to bring in talent from the East, the traditional Orient, a term that has fallen in disfavor. But to me, still has an exotic tone to it." He pointed to a large stage area. "Musicians, singers, comedians, Chinese Revolutionary Opera, even acrobatic acts. I have built this place to handle all of these."

Kim examined the entire area with a practiced eye. "Why so grand? Do you think the city will appreciate it?" she asked.

John laughed, then replied. "Seattle needs this. Bellevue and the outlying areas are beginning to attract people away to their entertainment venues."

John pointed out a large side picture window and explained. "Along that curb area will be a fleet of limos and top-of-the-line busses who will bring anyone who wishes here, for free. Once here, they will enjoy spending their money." He turned and looked into her eyes.

"This and 'The Jade Garden,' which I just purchased, are the beginning of an entertainment package I have planned. I am working with some of the local Native American Tribes to find a location where we can partner in a new Asian Casino. After all, Native Americans Tribes are cousins to the Asians, and Chinese. Why not reunite as our ancestors were?"

"You are quite the businessman, John," Kim commented. "And quite the nice dreamer."

John laughed again and spoke. "Without dreams, dear Kim, we are boring and slothful."

He clasped her hands in his and kissed them. "I've never enjoyed telling anyone my plans as much as I have enjoyed telling you," his voice husky. "I hope I may continue in that endeavor."

Kim gently removed a hand from John's grasp, reached up and used his silken tie to pull him closer. She kissed him deeply, feeling a warm stirring as he kissed back.

"Does that answer your question?" Kim said as they parted.

"Yes, it does my beauty," was the handsome man's reply.

The rest of the evening was a dream. In addition to a spirited auction, John had also arranged for a dance band. As the evening progressed, patrons could trip the light fantastic. During the ensemble of songs, a sudden Tango appeared. John held his hand out to Kim as he asked,

"Shall we, as I understand you are half Argentine?"

Kim almost grinned as she replied. "Is this a test of my mother's heritage? O ye of little faith!"

The *Lengha* was loose enough fit to allow many of the sweeps, strides and leg motions of the more intricate Argentine Tango, not the old Hollywood version. Kim soon discovered that John had more than just a passing knowledge of the dance. As they danced, the rest of the participants soon gave room to the couple, Kim and John seeming to be long time dance partners. He must have given some special instructions to the band leader as the Tango went on longer than most. Kim noticed but did not care, for this was the most fun she had experienced in years.

Then, it was over. As John held her in a final dance embrace, kissed the hand he clasped in his, applause broke out. Surprised to find her the center of attention, Kim blushed and tried to step behind John. He would have none of that.

"Allow these good people to pay homage to your dancing skills... and your beauty," John commanded.

"Agents want to stay in the background—" protested Kim.

"Tonight, you are Kim Kupar, exotic beauty representing India and Argentina," John replied. "Accept it."

Eventually, the applause slackened, and the couple left the dance floor. John steered them toward the long ornate bar for cool refreshment. And there Kim received another surprise.

"Akal! A.J! What are you doing working here?"

Her young brother, of slender build and barely taller than Kim, shyly smiled and replied.

"The Union said this was a high-end gig and they needed the best. So, here I am, Sister."

A.J. then noticed that John was standing behind

her, began to stutter.

"Mr. Wang. Sir! I hope everything is to your satisfaction..."

John stuck his hand out to shake. "I thought I saw a 'Kupar' on the casual labor list. Like your sister Kim, my guest, you are of superior abilities. No, don't blush. I watch all the employees. You have a fast yet relaxed way of serving the customers. I like that."

"Why, thank you, Sir! I..."

The business leader produced an ornate business card as he spoke.

"Here. My private line to my business office. Call me tomorrow if you'd like a permanent position."

A.J tried to stutter out more thanks, and Kim interrupted with a sisterly kiss on the cheek.

"I will call you tomorrow, Little Brother," she said in Punjabi. A.J slyly smiled.

"I think not, Kim," he answered. *"I will call you later. Enjoy yourself. You work too hard."*

Kim smiled back, tried not to blush. She and John collected their drinks and went to private table. After they found their seats, John reached across the table and took Kim's hands in a gentle grasp.

"You, my dear, are unlike anyone I have ever met," he said.

Kim met his gaze as she replied. "I've heard you have been with many, shall we say, unique women."

John chuckled, then replied. "Yes, I will not lie, especially to you. I've kept company with many pretty women. Some whose families felt I used, abused, and then threw them away."

"Did you, John?" Kim asked. "Use them?"

John paused for a moment, his look became

serious as he answered.

"I enjoyed their company as they, I believe, they enjoyed mine. Some of the enjoyment was physical. And, it was all voluntary." The Asian Business Association President cocked his head a bit. "Kim Kupar, you ask questions others only ponder about in private. I think I like your bluntness and aggressive search for the truth. I see you are an excellent criminal investigator, are a great addition to your Agency."

Kim presented John with a coy smile. "I bet you say that to all the girls," she said.

John laughed, with the same attractive sparkle in his eyes.

"I can honestly say you are the first law enforcement officer I have ever dined, danced, and drank with," he admitted. "If all female 'Cops' I believe is the generic term, are like you, I guess I have been missing out on a very unique class of potential dates."

"You mean I've now created competition for myself?" Kim asked coquettishly.

John kissed her hands again. "Never," he stated. "None can hold a candle to you."

They leaned across the table and kissed again. Kim knew that everything seemed to be happening so very fast. However, after many years of trying to weave through male and female relationships, this time with John felt so 'right.' Plus, he had saved her life.

John stood up. "Come," he said as he held out his hand. "I must complete another check of this event, ensure that everyone is happy and content. People who are happy and content come back with friends, and spend money."

Kim smiled. "You are the commensurate

businessman," she said. "Even while enjoying yourself, you have an eye on the bottom line."

John took her hand and helped her from her seat. He then pulled her to him, Kim liking the feel of his chest against her breasts.

"You, Kim," he said, "have taken my eyes from my bottom line and replaced it with a vision of your loveliness."

"Ever the flattering politician," whispered Kim.

"No flattery. The truth." They kissed again, both now in their own world. As their mouths parted, Kim nibbled at John's bottom lip. John laughed.

"Oh, you're full of surprises," he whispered.

"You forget, John, where the Kama Sutra was written," was Kim's reply

John gazed again into her eyes. Kim met his gaze, felt the sparks increase in intensity. He put an arm around her waist and began a stroll around the establishment.

"This will not take long, Kim. Then if you wish, we can be alone."

"I wish." The two words passed Kim's lips before she realized what she had said. But the warmth in her body told her it was what she wanted, this particular night.

As the strolled past the bar, Kim saw that A.J. was pouring a soft drink for a beautiful young Chinese female. When A.J. saw John Wang, he quickly blurted out.

"Just a soft drink for Miss Jade here. No alcohol."

John grinned. Then replied. "Of course. Like your sister, a stickler for what is right. Kim, let me introduce you to the cousin of a close family friend. Kim Kupar, please meet Jade Chang. I've been asked to watch over her, mentor her until her family can immigrate."

Kim saw the young Chinese female was beautiful nearing gorgeous, and seemed to be poured into the Asian dress with gold trimmings. Jet black below shoulder length hair, well brushed to shiny beauty, framed a pretty Chinese face with clear skin. Somewhat high cheekbones and a lovely, feminine nose by Chinese standards rounded out the attractive vision, which was Jade Chang. Even in the subdued bar lights, Kim also noticed another unique feature as the young lady bowed, then offered her hand to shake.

"Pleased to meet you, Ma'am," Jade said in accented English.

Kim smiled and replied in Mandarin. *"It is a pleasure to meet you. And we have something in common, we both have jade eyes."*

At both Kim's excellent Mandarin and the mention of 'jade eyes,' the young Chinese woman's (barely out of girlhood)eyes widened, and she looked at John. He laughed.

"Yes, Miss Kupar speaks better Mandarin than many Chinese. And she is also blessed with jade colored eyes."

Jade looked at Kim and smiled. "I am learning English, Miss Kim. Hopefully, I speak... well?"

Kim smiled again, patted Jades arm as she replied. "You are doing just fine. If John will let me, I'd be happy to help with your English."

"Let us get her settled with her other studies, dear Kim," John interjected. "She's here on a Student Visa right now. I have her employed here part-time as a traditional coat and hat check girl, or attendant as the 'P. C. Police' demands I call her."

"Mister Wang helps me," Jade added. "I am so new here—"

"Yes, of course, Jade. Now please run along. People will begin leaving soon."

Jade glanced at John, then bowed to him, then to Kim.

"It is a pleasure to meet you," Jade said to Kim.

"And I you. I hope to see you soon," replied Kim.

Jade backed up several steps in respect, then turned and hurried back to her duties. John looked at Kim.

"Well, what do you think of young Jade?" John asked.

"I think she is lucky to have a mentor and protector such as you in a strange land," answered Kim.

John raised his chin a bit, gazed across the business. "I guess I am her protector," he stated. Then he was back to smiling at and talking to Kim.

"Now, shall we, my dear? A.J."

"Sir!" Kim's brother called out

"Call me first thing Monday morning."

"Yes, Sir."

John walked Kim out to the line of limousines.

"So, John, you wish to put me in a limo and send me elsewhere?" Kim asked in a low and sultry voice.

"No!" John stated. "Of course not. The back of a limo will just provide us with a little quiet time together."

John opened the back door, motioning the nearby attendant that he had things under control. Kim felt her pulse begin to race as she turned around in the spacious rear seat area and smiled at John. Then they were both clinching in each other's arms as they kissed deeply and long. Kim felt John's hands begin to caress her bare legs, there had been no need for her to wear nylons to show off her young and shapely legs. John's hands reached up and caressed her thighs as Kim kneaded certain sensitive areas of the man's body. Kim heard herself moan as if someone else was making the earthy noise.

"My townhouse is nearby, John." It came out of her mouth before she realized she had said it.

John leaned back a bit, looked into her eyes. "Is that what—?"

Kim pulled him to her and began to nibble and bite on his neck.

"Yes." Kim paused long enough to answer. "You know my address."

"I do."

Kim stopped her ministries of John's neck. "The flowers were gorgeous," she said.

"As are you, my jade eyed beauty," responded John.

"You say that to all the girls in the back seat of a limo, don't you?" Kim asked playfully.

John took her face in his strong hands. "No." His answer was strong and sure. He paused long enough to give the address to the drive in the front seat, then buried his face in Kim's substantial and sweat moistened breasts.

"My Lord," Kim whispered as she wrapped her strong legs around the subject of her desire and pulled him into her body.

10.

K im was unsure of the time as she laid next to John, her head on his strong shoulder. She gently scratched his chest with her jade-colored fingernails as she regaled in his manly scent. They had made love for quite some time, so Kim knew it was early Saturday morning. No need to rush to the office, no need to do much of anything, other than lay in her bed next to John. She heard John's stomach gurgle a bit, and she smiled.

"Typical male. Hungry after love," she opined. She rose up on one arm and looked at her lovers face. "My mother said that if you kept a man satiated in his two areas of appetite, his stomach, and an organ a bit south of that, a woman could keep him forever."

John turned his head and smiled at her, then replied. "And you have found this to be so in your worldly experience?"

Kim paused for a moment, then answered. "I guess yes and no. I have experienced-physical love, of course. But I've never had a true long term relationship with a man. Much to the frustration of my mother."

John turned toward Kim and kissed her lips. He nuzzled her neck, caressed her breasts. Kim's breathing quickened, and she ran her fingers through his black and well-groomed hair. She next moved one hand down John's body to the 'southern organ' her mother had mentioned. John let out a soft groan.

"How I ever missed the study of the Kama Sutra..." said John.

Kim giggled, something she had not done in years. "First lesson," she said. "This, part of you, is referred to as a *lingam*. I have a *yonis*—"

The sun well above the horizon when Kim put the finishing touches on an "American Breakfast', bacon, eggs, hash browns, and toast. John sat at her table, smiling as she prepared a plate for him.

"I thought many East Indians were vegetarians," John commented.

Kim smiled at him as she placed the food in front of John.

"My father's side of the family, many are still traditional Sikhs," she said. "So yes, they are basically vegetarian. But he takes the equivalent of a 'reformed' stance, like Reformed Jews. The belief in the spiritual teachings of the Gurus is what is essential, not following some ancient list of dietary and dress prohibitions."

Kim chuckled, then continued. "Besides, my mother loves Argentine beef. No way would she become a vegetarian."

John laughed, picked up his silverware. "So, your mother is Christian?"

"Catholic," Kim replied. "Thus, she is quite good at 'Roman Guilt' as some have called it. I frustrate her with my lack of attending Mass, as I disappoint my father with not following even the basic teachings of the Gurus."

"I must be nosey and ask," John said. "How did two from such different cultures meet and fall in love?"

Kim sat her own plate down next to John and began to eat and explain.

"One of the great unsung love stories. They met at an Electronics and Computer Convention. Not only was my mother a whiz with computers, but she had model looks. So, a major company was using her as eye-candy at a large product booth. My father had already started building his import and export business, went to the booth to look at new products."

Kim laughed as she continued with the story. "My mother says my father was so smitten he kept stuttering and dropping things. He claims she kept following him around, would not leave him alone. I think it was someplace in the middle."

"But they fell in love there," John asked.

"Yes. Married six months later," answered Kim. "The two families had some trouble accepting this union of two very different cultures. Well, different in their eyes, anyway."

John sipped the tea Kim had brewed. "You see a lot of similarities?" He continued in his questioning.

Kim answered between bites I food. "Both are conservative in the idea of man-woman relationships. They want people to marry, women will have babies, raise them to be fine examples to carry on the family name."

"And you?" John asked as he fixed his gaze on Kim. Kim looked up, locked eyes with him. She stopped eating, stood up, and moved over to John. She had put an apron on to protect her soft parts while cooking but wore nothing else. The Asian businessman wore nothing. John pushed his chair back, and Kim sat on his lap. They kissed for over a minute.

"Someday, I want a family," answered Kim. "Now, I guess I am 'in the moment' with you."

"And this moment will last—?"

Kim gazed into his dark eyes. "Have any plans for the rest of the weekend?" she asked.

"Not until late Sunday," was John's answer. "And you, my dear?"

"Ditto," was her reply. "Though I was thinking of some more cross-cultural instruction."

"Hmm. Kim, you mean, what is rising to the occasion is a *lingam*—?

"Yes. And a *yonis* awaits."

11.

Monday seemed to come much too soon. However, duty called, and Kim was in the SAC office bright and early. Now she frowned as she looked over a report she had received from the staff at the Zoology Department at the Woodland Park Zoo. Attached to it was a supplemental prepared by the U.S. Fish and Wildlife Department.

"Here you go, young lady. Tea and a Fat Pill." Rex interrupted her examination of the reports with the offered refreshments. She flashed a broad smile at Rex.

"Thanks, Rex," she said. "I can use the sugar of a fattening donut."

Rex smirked as he spoke. "I can imagine. What with all the exercise—"

"You know, you are about to wear this tea," Kim warned.

"Oh, alright. Just my rude and crude sense of humor. No offense meant."

Kim sat her tea down, softly patted his arm.

"None taken," she assured the mature Agent. "You brought me luck, and have introduced me to a lot of fascinating people. Just remember I'm a 'big girl,' can take care of myself."

Rex paused, gave her a serious look before he spoke.

"Sorry. The traditionalist in me keeps wanting to treat you like a daughter. But, you're a daughter who could kick my ass."

"Which I will never do," Kim again assured him. "Now, I've a bit of a conundrum."

"You mean a mystery. Thar yah go again with them big words," Rex said in a backwoods accent.

Kim shook her head, smiled, then continued. "This report on the dead panda says the examiners of the body found what I thought they would. A panda with signs of genetic manipulation, cloning. But...."

"A big but, right?" said Rex. "Like you find on the Internet—"

"Rex. Concentrate. What they found was some other hair and flesh samples that did not match the panda's," Kim explained

"And not human either, right, Kim?"

"Yes, Sir. We have fur and cells from a large feline. It looks like Bengal Tiger, but—" she stopped in her explanation.

"There is that big 'but' again," prompted Rex.

Kim frowned and continued. "Yes. First, why a tiger with a panda? Second, this is no normal Bengal. They did something to it. It's going to take a while for the zoologists to figure out."

"Well," interjected Rex. "To cut to the chase, they smuggled in tigers and other animals. Plus people."

"Yes, Rex. Why the mixture? Why not concentrate on one commodity? Why complicate things?"

Rex picked up the file, scanned it. He handed it pack to Kim and explained.

"Smugglers smuggle. Whatever turns a big profit. It would seem logical to specialize, make things easier. However, smuggling has existed for as long as people have been in America. Some of the means and tactics have remained the same for decades, just the items smuggled change."

"You've seen this before?" Kim asked.

"Yep." Rex then explained, "A friend of mine had a case in the Florida Keys. A group run by a woman smuggled computers and electronics into Cuba, parrots, and drugs from Cuba into the U.S. And, they would take people both ways also. Used high speed 'go-fast' boats in both directions."

Kim perused the report some more, sipped her tea.

"What's next, Kim? Whatta want to do, Case Agent?" Rex asked.

"Mind a trip to the Zoo?" said Kim.

"Hell, I love Woodland Park. As long as we can stop by the Monkey House," Rex replied.

Kim frowned. "Why the monkeys?" she asked Rex. He explained.

"Why, to look up a couple of my former supervisors, that's why."

12.

WOODLAND PARK ZOO, SEATTLE

About an hour later, Kim and Rex were waiting outside the Big Cat, AKA Feline section of the Zoo. Kim enjoyed the familiar pungent smell of large predators that wafted from the enclosure. She had done some internship work in this section while getting her Graduates Degree, still had both two-legged and four legged old friends here.

"You worked here?" Rex asked.

"Internship," Kim replied. "While getting my graduates degree."

Rex looked at her, grunted. "I guess the big cats can sense you have a connection," he said.

Kim shrugged. "Maybe," she answered. "Lions are a pride, more social of the cats, so they are easier to understand. A Bengal? A loner, other than when it comes time for mating. Even then, they seem to beat the crap out of each other to show their love and affection. Actually, just shows how horny the male is and the female wants to see if he is strong enough to be worthy of producing offspring with her. No dinner and dancing for them."

Rex laughed, then commented.

"Well, that would make it a lot simpler for us if we humans had definite mating seasons."

Kim gave a wry smile.

"Yes, but there is that theory that us, being nasty and horny monkeys, caused humans to push the envelope, develop fire, and so on," she explained. "Our sex drive drove us to evolve, advance."

"Might have something there, Kim," Rex agreed. "Men push women for sex, and women push us, men, to do something more if we want any affection. Short of taking it by force. But then, we have to sleep sometime. And the ole Bobbitt Syndrome rears its ugly head."

At that moment a young very well-built and traditionally handsome blond haired man walked out from the enclosure, greeted Kim with a broad grin and a husky voice.

"About time you came back to visit, Kim!"

Kim walked up to him, and they hugged as she asked, "How are you doing, Hank?"

The man named Hank stepped back to reply. "Missing you, that's how I'm doing. And I see you brought a friend."

"Hank Thomas, say hello to Senior Special Agent Rex Moyer. He's my,"

"Partner," Rex jumped in. He shook Hank's hand, "So you handle the 'Big Cats.' That must be interesting."

Hank laughed, then explained. "Hell, they handle us. You screw up around a predatory feline, they won't eat your lunch, you become lunch. I bench press a lot, but I'd be a toy in the grips of a tiger or lion."

Hank touched Kim's arm as he asked, "So, how can I help you?"

"I read the report you and the Zoo put together. Just how modified was the Bengal?"

Hank paused, then answered. "We called the sample something from the Bengal group, but it was so modified that it might just as well be from some 'Triassic Park' DNA lab. A Bengal Tiger just seemed to be the closest existing big cat we could come up with."

"How could you tell with a small sample?" Rex asked.

"Because it was so damned *weird*," was Hank's reply. "It's like something from a science fiction 'B' movie. Way too much gene splicing. I'm surprised the specimen could exist outside a laboratory."

Kim frowned as she asked, "Why? I mean, why create such a strange creature?"

Hank shrugged in his reply. "The only thing I can figure out is the damn Chinese are trying to breed even more exotic animals for sale on the black-market. They already try to sell to zoos like Woodland Park cubs they claim were recovered from the wild due to dead mothers. But we know they were bred or cloned in some damn animal farm."

Rex looked at Hank. "You're pissed," he said

"Hell Yes!" The comment burst from Hank. "They are fucking with Mother Nature. Whenever we 'monkeys' do this, we invariably create monsters. Mules are bad enough, but some of the photos I've seen smuggled out—" He began to shake with rage. Kim stepped close and rubbed his back.

"Hey, Big Man. It's okay," she reassured him. "We're on your side."

Hank took a deep breath, let it out.

"Sorry. I guess I have a love affair with big cats, wolves, all the major predators. A 'Bambi' guy I'm not."

"Kim, give him one of your business cards. Hank, could you call us if you get any more feelers from China?" Rex asked. "If someone tries to market some cubs, maybe we can get with Fish and Wildlife, set up a sting."

Hanks face lit up, his voice now controlled. "Yeah? We've been trying to get this on someone's radar screen forever!" He looked at Kim. "Now I don't feel so bad losing you to the Feds. Rex, is it? Stop by anytime. Bring any kids you have. Friend of Kim is a friend of mine. Hell, everyone here misses you, Kim."

Kim blushed looked away. Hank grabbed and hugged her as he spoke with new enthusiasm.

"Gotta get back to work. You keep up the good fight. You two just made my day!"

The two Special Agents made their way back to Kim's Mustang. As they took their seats in the vehicle, Rex cleared his throat.

"Ah, can't help myself. I have to ask. You and Hank had a bit of a 'thing' going on?"

Kim paused, sighed, and answered. "Yeah. Is it still that obvious? Damn."

"What's the matter? Everyone has Exes. Even an old ugly guy like me," Rex admitted.

Kim's mouth formed a sad smile, then she spoke. "He loved me. A lot. But when I said I was going to apply for a law enforcement job, then was picked up by DHS, ICE, all Hell broke loose. He thought I was picking a job and career change over him."

"Well, you were," Rex stated succinctly.

Kim turned quick and stared at Rex. "What? That's

kind of rough to say!" She almost spat out her reply.

Rex looked at Kim. "You realize how many guys have done that?" Rex asked. "Moved away, went into the Military, whatever, and left some sweetheart behind? Welcome to the world of equal rights with men."

Kim sat, in silence, a bit stunned.

"Look it, Kim. I'm sorry I was so blunt. I don't want—"

"Its fine, T-Rex. You're right," Kim interrupted Rex's explanation. "Blunt, rude, crude, and socially unacceptable like you say, but right." She looked at him and smiled.

"Thanks for being, I think the old expression was, a Dutch Uncle. I think I needed someone to point out the obvious."

"Okay. And with that, I guess I owe you lunch," Rex suggested. "But not Chinese. I think you probably have your fill of that."

Kim's mouth fell open, and she stared at T-Rex. Then it dawned on Rex Moyer what he had said, and he began to blush. A lot.

"Shit! That came out wrong. What I meant was that we have been hanging around Chinatown, I mean Chinese businesses. I—. Oh, Fuck!" The former Border Agent tried to hide his head under his jacket. Kim began to laugh. Then belly laugh. Then guffaw. She laughed so hard tears were streaming down her face.

"Oh, that's right," Rex said from under his jacket, his voice muffled. "Make fun of ole T-Rex. I can take it."

After a few ending hiccups, Kim brought herself under control. She bent the rear view mirror so she could see how much damage her light makeup had sustained.

"Well, Rex. A few touch-ups to my face and we'll

go," Kim finally said.

"Okay. Can you stop and find me a paper bag? I need to hide my face."

"Oh, quit that. Now, what do you want to eat?" Kim asked.

"Japanese? Sushi? I mean, you haven't had your fill of the Asian cuisine. Just Chinese." As soon as he said it, he knew he was in deep *Kimchee.*

Kim looked at him, began to laugh again. "Damn it, Kim. Stop that! God, find some duct tape in the back. I'll just tape my mouth shut."

13.

Kim slammed the heavy hitting bag with a hard right knee, then followed with an equally hard left knee. She danced back, jabbing with her hands at the now moving bag. The SAC Office had built a state of the art work out room during a remodel a few years ago. Kim and other Agents made good use of it, saving themselves the added expense of a downtown Seattle gym membership. As the younger Special Agents soon found out, nothing was inexpensive in downtown Seattle.

Kim stepped back and stopped, getting her breathing back in control before launching another attack on the stand-in for an opponent. An excellent physical workout after many hours trying to put two and two together in the Trafficking case helped to work the kinks out in both her body and her mind. Rex was doing his best on an incline bicycle, also building up a sweat. "Gotta keep the old Grim Reaper at bay," he had told her the other day. Kim knew that underneath his beer gut, there was some healthy muscle, but he needed cardio to keep his heart halfway healthy.

"Ah, the smell of female sweat. Love it."

The loud voice, of course, drew Kim's attention. It belonged to one Don Johnson, a large and dark-skinned African American Special Agent who believed he was God's gift to the female gender. He was another former "jock' who had thought he was going to have a career in the NFL. College ball disbursed him of that belief when he discovered he was not 'that good.' He had a chip on his shoulder ever since. Unlike Dennis Spain, who had some talent and accepted the fact it was not enough for a Pro career, Johnson always talked about how he was 'screwed.' Thus, he wound up being recruited by DHS out of college, attitude, and all, as he had no other prospects.

Dennis Spain, who tried to be friendly with him as a 'Bro,' jumped in before the conversation really started as he followed the other Agent into the workout are.

"Hey, Don. Let's not get crude."

"Hey, Man. Just joking around. You can take a joke, right, Kim?" Don asked.

Kim presented him with a slight smile as she replied. "Yes, I enjoy humor. Good humor."

This elicited a guffaw from Rex on the recline bike. Don shot a glare at him.

"What's so funny, Old Man?" he challenged.

"Not your jokes, that's for sure," replied Rex.

"Come on, Don. Let's get a good work out in," said Dennis. He started to take Don's arm, but the man jerked it away.

"Hey, I think Kim needs a workout partner, not you!" He stared at Kim.

"What do you say? I'd be better sparring partner than that heavy bag," claimed the large man.

"I wouldn't do that if I were you," interjected Rex.

"If I want your opinion, I'll squeeze your head!" Don spat back.

Don Johnson walked up toward Kim at the heavy bag. "Come on," he said. "I heard you're a real badass on the street, kicked some Chinese ass."

"Don, dammit..." Dennis said.

"Hey, no sweat, buddy. Kim and I will just go a few rounds. Whatta say, Honey?" Don Johnson asked with a sneer.

Kim frowned. "I don't think this is a—" she began to say.

"Don't be a wimp, girly," Don stated as he stepped forward and made an open-handed slap at Kim's face, a grin that looked more like a leer on his face. It never landed.

Kim blocked the slap and came up with a high extended front kick which *Kalaripayattu* was known for in the martial arts community. Kim's right foot caught the aggressive Agent under his chin, snapping his head back. The big man toppled back as if poleaxed, only the mat material around the heavy bag keeping Don's head from smashing hard on the bare floor.

"Shit!" Rex said as he scrambled up from the recline bike. Both he and Dennis were next to the prone Don as he began to moan.

Kim pulled her workout gloves off. "I didn't mean that to happen! It was just reflex," said Kim. She stepped over to the moaning Agent. "I'm sorry..."

"It's his fault, Kim," said Dennis. "This isn't the first time some woman smacked him for being a smartass. Usually, it's in a bar."

"Get a wet towel, Kim," Rex ordered as he looked

at the head of the fallen Agent. "The mat kept him from a cracked skull. But he may have a bit of a concussion."

Kim came back with the wet towel, and Don began to come around with the application of the wet towel by Rex.

"What…" Don mumbled.

"You slipped and fell on your ass screwing around with Kim. Got it?" Rex's tone was commanding, not suggesting.

"What? She—" Don tried to say.

"She kicked your ass after you tried to hit her," The Senior Agent cut in. "Want to talk to OPR, Internal Affairs, explain that one?"

"Yeah, Don. I'm not covering for you here," Dennis added.

Rex and Dennis helped Don to his feet as the man glared at Kim.

"This ain't over—" Don tried to growl at Kim.

Rex stepped in, an inch from the taller man's face.

"Yes, it is!" Rex barked at him. "Because if you fuck with my partner, you fuck with me. And this fat old man doesn't take prisoners."

Don saw the steel in his gaze, knew that Rex was not one to cross.

"Let me go," Don snarled as he pushed the two men back and huffed from the room. Kim looked at Dennis and Rex.

"I'm sorry that—" started Kim.

"Will you please stifle that, Agent?" Rex snapped. "He tried to lay hands on you because he's a basic bully. If I was as limber as you, I'd done the same."

"I'm still sorry, Sir." Kim stuck her chin out in defiance as she replied to the rebuke by her Training

Agent. She was angry at Don and herself for being in the situation. However, she had been trained not to suffer any abuse from others.

"Agent Spain, please take Agent Kupar here and buy her a tea," Rex requested.

"Alright, Rex. Kim—"

"Dammit, I do not need to be babied!" Kim shot back.

"This is not being babied," the Senior Agent replied. "It's covering your ass. Now, don't argue." There was a steely coldness in Rex's voice she had never heard before. Still angry, she allowed Dennis to take her downstairs to street level and buy her a hot tea.

Kim stood, still angry, sipped her tea as Dennis Spain stood quietly by. He knew Kim well enough to know she would talk when she felt like it. Finally, she found her voice.

"There is no reason to treat me as some little girl that needs to be protected. I decked Don, I'm willing to accept the consequences. I wear women pants, not little girl panties!" Kim fumed. She had not been this angry in a while. Even the Longshoremen had not made her this pissed off.

Dennis snorted, then commented. "You just don't get T-Rex, do you?"

"What do you mean?" Asked Kim.

"He treats everyone this way," explained Dennis. "At least all of us younger Agents he has helped train. We are all under his wing from time to time."

"Well, I'm not some chick that needs a momma hen to protect her!" Protested Kim. "I'm—"

"A grown woman who is a badass and be damned, we menfolk had better not forget it. Right?" For the first time, Dennis, her close friend, had an edge to his voice. She studied his face.

"You're mad at me," Kim said.

Dennis took a deep breath, let it out before he spoke.

"I'm mad at the situation. And myself for letting Don to be such a dick around me. I should call him on his crap more often. But I know he is not the most popular black man around."

"You're his friend," Kim declared. "So you try not to hurt him."

"Sometimes, a true friend tells the person what they don't want to hear," Dennis replied.

"And," Kim added. "Sometimes, a true friend is loyal to a fault."

Dennis chuckled. "Wise beyond your years, Kim. So I hope I can count you as a friend."

Kim touched his hand. "Of course, which is why I don't want to anger you."

"Water off a ducks back. Besides, Like I said. I'm angry with myself."

At that moment, Rex walked up. "So, who gets to buy me coffee?"

"If it will sweeten your disposition, I will," Kim said.

Rex snorted. "Well, I just had a little discussion with Salmon. So, I need some sweetening up!"

"Senior Agent Moyer..."

"What? All formal now?"

Kim sighed. "I'm just trying to apologize for causing problems—"

"God, you are so hard headed. Did I not tell you there is nothing to apologize for? Now, I need to drain a certain part of my anatomy while you get me my coffee." Rex turned and strode off.

Kim looked at Dennis, her face a picture of frustration.

"Look, Kim," Dennis explained. "Rex does what he does. He took the heat with Salmon, probably told Don that if he pushed it, he'd make damn sure there was a formal complaint about laying hands on a female Agent. So, Salmon will say nothing happened, forget it, or else. At the same time, he fumes at Rex, blames him for bringing the problem to him. Even though that is Salmon's job, handling problems between Agents."

Kim paused in thought before she answered. "So he has been doing this, 'handling' problems of other Agents for a long time."

"Yep. Which is why he was never made a supervisor. Rex has a tendency of pissing management off by telling them how to handle problems."

Not for the first time did Kim think about the contradiction that was 'T-Rex.' He had a reputation as this hard case individual, profane, and a bit of a curmudgeon at times. Yet, he was quick to jump to the defense of others. She walked over as she was in thought and purchased Rex's coffee. When she walked back to Dennis, Rex had returned.

"Ah, coffee. The elixir for all Cops," Rex said as he took the coffee from her. He sipped it. "I'm addicted to this mocha flavor though. When I started, you were lucky to get flavored cream."

Dennis had slid off to the Men's Room, leaving Kim and Rex alone.

"Rex..."

"You start to apologize again, and I will be angry.

And you do not want to see me angry."

Kim smiled. "Are you going to turn green and expand until your clothes rip off?" she asked.

At that comment, Rex chuckled. "Well, my wife is claiming I'm gaining too much weight."

He sighed, then began again. "Look, I had a little talk with Salmon and Don to derail this from going anywhere. You rung the man's chimes good. But it's his fault for being a smartass. However, any physical violence between Agents is greatly frowned upon. So, a little talking, listening to Salmon complain and act all supervisory, and the problem is swept under the rug. Especially since Salmon wants nothing to interfere with his transfer to D.C."

Kim stood in thought for a moment. Then she said, "Thanks. I think I owe you one."

"De Nada, young lady. Shit happens, as they say among us more profane Agents."

Rex sipped his coffee, then looked at his watch. "Go shower, clean up," directed Rex. "Then we do a little more snooping around."

"Yes, Sir."

"There you go again. Mixing me up with my father."

14.

It was a bit past seven in the evening when Kim arrived at her townhouse. She turned her security system off, entered, set her carrying case, gym bag, and jacket down, and then plunked down on her overstuffed sofa.

"Ufff," she said to herself. After the gym 'incident,' she and Rex had done some snooping around Chinatown, talking to some locals who knew Rex well. Now, however, many met Kim with a big smile, especially when they found out she spoke Chinese like a native. It seemed to fascinate some of the older women that a young and attractive female as her had the authority and responsibility of a Federal Agent. Some of the local women from all the Asian groups seemed to want Kim to talk to their younger daughters, explain the opportunities the United States offered for females not available in their native and more conservative homelands.

Kim stretched her entire body out on the sofa, trying her best cat imitation. On the verge of purring, her cellphone range.

"Kim here," answered Kim.

"Hey, Sis. You busy?" It was A.J. on the other end. She sat up, smiling.

"A.J! What's up? Usually, its months before I hear from you."

"Well, I thought I'd come over and see you, now that I have a definite full-time gig at the 'Jade Palace,'" said A.J. "By the way, thanks for helping grease it with Mister Wang."

"A.J. I didn't even know you were working there until that night,' Kim replied.

"Well, you liking the Boss, and him liking you, did not hurt."

Kim tried to keep an even tone. "Who said I liked him."

A.J. began to laugh at the other end of the phone, and Kim was glad he could not see her grin.

"Hey, remember this is your younger brother you are talking to. Anyways, can I come over? I'll bring some take out, some wine."

"Yeah, sure. Come on over," Kim said. "I need a laid back night."

"Be there in a few, Sis."

"I'll buzz you up, A.J."

Some twenty minutes later, Kim now in a clean set of pink sweats, let her little brother in, gave him a big sisterly hug.

"Ooof! Don't bruise the ribcage, Sis!" A.J. was slight of build but had a charm and attractiveness that all the women his age found irresistible.

"Oh quit you faking!" Kim ordered. "I can feel your muscles under that shirt, A.J."

Within moments, they were sitting on the sofa, food on the coffee table, stuffing their faces.

In between bites, A.J asked. "So how's the job going?"

Kim swallowed, then answered. "Great. I'm even getting used to my fill-in Training Agent called T-Rex."

"T-Rex? Why that name?"

"Because Rex is like an old dinosaur who snaps and growls a lot," Kim replied. "But he's a good man."

A.J. laughed, "Well, I have to admit the rest of us in the family get concerned when we hear about fights and shootings. Sure, you are safe enough?"

"Hey, Brother," Kim retorted. "Our father and the rest of the family taught us to take care of ourselves. Not to mention that I have a whole office of other Agents as back up."

"True. But brothers always worry about sisters," A.J. said. "We guys always have an urge to, you know, protect the women in our lives."

Kim smiled slyly at A.J. "Well, do you have a woman in your life? Other than your sister and mother, that is?"

A.J actually blushed a bit under his natural tan as he replied. "Maybe. Kinda. It's kind of complicated."

"Well, tell your Big Sister. I'm all ears," she quipped.

Her brother paused for a moment, seemed to choose his words carefully.

"That young Chinese lady you met, the hat and coat check girl at the 'Palace.' She likes to hang around me a lot. And-I like her. She definitely loves that I speak Mandarin."

Kim frowned a bit. "She's kind of young,"

she observed.

"Jade says she's eighteen," A.J.- replied. "The way she dresses for the nightclub she looks older. But Mr. Wang told me not to serve her alcohol if she asks."

"What does John, um, Mr. Wang say about it, her hanging around you?"

"He acts like an older brother, keeps an eye on her. She definitely kowtows to him when he talks to her."

"Has he said anything to you?" Questioned Kim.

"No," her brother answered. "But I can tell how far I can go in my position. I'm not wet behind the ears when it comes to dealing with bosses. So, on the job, I don't push it. However, I am trying to find a way to see her away from work."

A.J. frowned, then added. "Get a jive from Jade that she is... hiding something, not telling the whole story."

"Come on, Little Brother. She may just be nervous about being in a foreign land.

"Yeah, you could be right. But can I ask you a serious question?"

Kim paused and examined her brother's face. He seemed genuinely concerned about something dealing with Jade. And, A.J. was not noted for having 'serious concerns' about much of anything.

"You can ask me anything, A.J. You know that."

"Well, Kim, what if Jade is here illegally?" A.J questioned. "What if she was smuggled in?"

Kim froze for a moment. She better than most people knew that human trafficking from China was rife up and down the West Coast. But John Wang hiring an Illegal Alien? Kim did not think he would risk his position in the community by hiring illegal workers.

"Tell you what, Little Brother. Leave the investigations to me,' Kim warned. "Don't bite off more than you can chew, as they say."

"I won't. But let's say Jade was—"

"Then I deal with it, not you," Kim retorted. "And if she was smuggled in by some Snakehead, she will be seen more as a victim than a criminal. The fact she wound up in John's care may be more of a blessing than if she were working for some massage parlor, giving 'happing endings' to middle-aged men."

A.J.s mouth dropped open a bit, then he closed it. "I keep forgetting what you do, the world you're in now. I keep thinking about you working in a lab, not the so-called mean streets of Seattle."

Kim chuckled and continued. "Yes, I'm getting quite the education. But back to the point. If this Jade does have a problem, I can probably help her with it, get some asylum or something for being a Trafficking Victim. So, don't became fixated on it, start worrying. Just worry about doing a good job at the Jade Palace."

A.J. smirked a bit, waved Kim's last comment away.

"Sis, I can do a good job there standing on my head."

"Well, if you stand on your head, I don't think the customers will want you serving drinks with your feet," quipped Kim.

A.J. let out a small laugh. "Okay, I get the point. Don't worry, be happy. Big Sister is watching out for me, as usual."

Kim reached over and hugged him, then kissed his cheek.

"Can't help being Big Sister, it's in my genes."

"I know-So, arm wrestle for the last spicy chicken wing?" Queried A.J.

"Why?" And with that, Kim snatched it and plunked it into her mouth.

"Hey, no fair!" her brother protested.

Kim sucked the meat off the bone.

"Too slow, my good man."

A.J. gave her a sly smirk. "So, I take it a certain Chinese businessman knows all about how quick you are with your mouth?" sassed A.J. And with that, he jumped from the sofa as Kim tried to smack him.

"Just wait when I catch you, A.J.!" Kim loudly warned.

"Too slow, Big Sister! Too slow!" A.J. retorted as he dashed about the townhouse, with his sister in full pursuit.

15.

OFFICE OF THE SPECIAL AGENT IN CHARGE
DHS/ICE, SEATTLE

K im was deep into studying the linkage charts and diagrams the ICE Intelligence Analysts had come up with. Smart Special Agents quickly learned to use and respect the work the Intelligence Analysts could produce. Using computer programs and databases like LEXUS NEXUS, the Analysts helped to develop a 'picture' in the form of a 'Link Chart' (as they were officially called) which showed the interconnections of all subjects and places in an investigation. Unfortunately, on the chart Kim was studying, there were still many linkage spheres with the words 'unknown subject' or 'unknown location.' Trying to figure out how exotic animal and human smuggling was connected with the alleged Snakehead group operating around the Port of Seattle was giving her eye strain.

Her cell phone rang, and she answered it in a distracted manner, her eyes and mind still on the computer screen.

"Agent Kupar."

"Hello, Kim. Working hard, I can tell." It was John Wang. Immediately her face broke into a broad smile. She switched to speaking in Mandarin.

"*John. So very nice to hear your voice. Sorry, I have not been able to get back to you, but—*"

"*You are submerged all the way up to your beautiful posterior in a certain smuggling investigation.*"

Kim almost giggled. How this man made her feel like a school girl talking to the football quarterback was beyond her intellectual understanding. But her emotional part just accepted and enjoyed it.

"*You could say that, John. Now, what prompted this pleasurable interruption?*" she queried.

"*As are you, I have been very busy with my businesses, not to mention with the Association,*" he replied. "*However, I am trying to block out some time to see you.*"

Kim leaned back in her office chair, trying to organize her schedule in her mind as she answered.

"*Possibly this weekend, dear one. I have missed you-all about you.*"

John chuckled, on the other end of the phone line. "*As I have you, my Jade Eyed Beauty. So, I must work late Friday and Saturday Night at the 'Jade Palace' but afterward—*"

"How about I pick my favorite Chinese businessman at closing time, take you to my place for a nightcap?" Kim suggested.

"And breakfast in bed?" John asked.

Kim felt a familiar warm feeling at the thought. "*I have a feeling that is an almost foregone conclusion. You get to cook this time.*"

John laughed. *"Then, it is settled. See you Friday Night."*

Kim made a little kissing sound over the phone, which seemed so high school. However, she could not help herself.

"I will return that kiss when I see you, Kim."

"Promise?" she replied.

"Yes. Trust me. Now I must go. Business calls."

Kim ended the call with a broad smile on her face. He made her feel so very lovely inside.

Then she heard a familiar voice down the hall that had been absent from the office. She left her desk chair in a flash and made a beeline down the hall.

"Matt! Matt Swenson!" Kim called out.

At the end of the office hallway, talking to Rex, was a tall thirty-something blond and handsome Matt. The Senior Special Agent flashed a broad grin at Kim as she approached.

Matt greeted her. "I see you are still in one piece, Kim, despite working with T-rex here."

The two Agents shook hands, then Matt gave her a quick hug. "My wife Pat wants you to stop by, so she can show the new little one off to you."

"Why, of course!" Kim replied. "When I'm not so busy, I'll offer my services as a babysitter."

"Don't say that too loud, Kim," warned her Mentor. "You'd be surprised the premium you pay for decent childcare."

Kim laughed. "But I will be free. I enjoy children."

"Yeah, other people's children are the best," interjected Rex. "You can leave them at their home when you get frustrated."

Matt patted Rex's shoulder. "Come on now. You

love your kids. And you are great at the Christmas Party every year."

"Hey, don't spread rumors," instructed Rex. "I have a reputation for a grouchy demeanor to uphold."

The small group of friends laughed for a moment, enjoyed a joyful distraction from their work. Rex looked at Matt with a e serious expression.

"So, I guess you'll come back, take this youngin' off my hands, take over her training," Rex asked.

"Hell, I heard you're doing a bang up job. Besides, it's not up to me. Salmon will have to decide when I come back to work on Monday."

T-Rex frowned. "Hey, I'm supposed to be a ROAD Agent by know," he protested.

Kim gave Matt a quizzical look. "ROAD? What does that stand for?"

Matt grinned. "Retired On Active Duty," he informed her."A term adopted from the Military. But, my fine T-Rex, I think circumstances dictate you keep working rather than goofing off."

"That's not fair!" The Senior Agent protested. "Here all these past months, I looked forward to sitting with my feet up, telling war stories to all the new Agents as they stumble in."

"No rest for the wicked, my friend," Matt replied. Now, you two can join me as I check my agent's mailbox for all the crap that has been accumulating these past weeks."

As the three Agents walked to the square opened mailboxes near the office entrance, one per assigned personnel, they noticed that someone had taped a folded piece of paper to the front of Kim's inbox. She frowned as she saw the word "Raptor" written on it.

"What is—" Kim unfolded the paper. Inside was a color picture of a Raptor dinosaur straight from the favorite movies about a particular island where such creatures existed. Rex grinned, and Matt began to chuckle.

"What does this mean?" Kim asked with a bit of a confused look.

"You, young lady, have just been christened."

"What do you mean? Christened? How?"

"Nickname, a Handle," interjected Matt. "A tradition of the Military as well as Cops. People in those careers love to tag people with unofficial names. Some more flattering than others. Raptor's not bad, in the greater scheme things."

Kim looked at Rex. "You didn't—" she began.

"Have anything to do with this?" Rex responded. "No. But just like I received my handle of T-Rex, you are now Raptor."

"But why this... creature. I mean, I have a background and affinity for the Big Cats—"

Rex laughed. "Raptors are alleged to have had the ability to kick-ass and take names," observed Rex. "I seem to remember a few instances, including one here in this office, where a certain young female Agent showed her ability to do just that."

Kim stuttered and blushed. She was used to being Kim, short for Kimberly, never had a real nickname. She always tried to blend in, not draw attention to herself, which was sometimes confusing due to her mixed race heritage.

Matt smiled at her. "Hey, it's not a bad name," he advised. "It does denote a being of speed and power."

"And," interjected Rex. "If you make too much of

a fuss about it, you may get tagged with a worse one."

"But a lizard—" Kim protested.

"No, a dinosaur," he informed Kim. "With the term 'raptor' that also applies to modern-day eagles and hawks. Besides, I'm called T-rex after a dinosaur. So what is so wrong with it?"

Kim sighed, then smiled. Best not to push it and risk insulting Rex. Being a 'dinosaur' at her young age was not something to which she had aspired.

"Well, Rex, I guess I will accept what I cannot change. Especially since you put it that way."

Rex grinned. "Good," he stated with finality. "Now, it's coffee time. Matt, you have time to have some, get caught up on the comings and goings in this fine establishment?"

Matt laughed. "Yeah, since you put it that way," he answered. "Pat's mother is at the house, helping out, so I've got some extra time."

Rex's grinned. "Just wait until I tell you all the goings on of Young Raptor here," he informed his friend.

"Rex..." Kim began.

"Oh, alright. Agent Kupar here. She is kicking ass and taking names in this human trafficking investigation."

Kim grit her teeth a bit. This could be a long day.

16.

THE JADE PALACE, SEATTLE

Kim pulled up to the valet parking at the nightclub in her Yaris two-door sedan. Her father and mother had frowned when she bought such an unassuming vehicle. Why not a BMW or some other high-end vehicle? Kim had told them there was no reason for such a car in the crowded streets of Seattle. She had her G-Ride, and larger vehicle would just lead to more parking problems. The valet quickly went into action when he saw Kim was driving the Yaris.

"Good evening, Miss Kupar."

"Good evening. If I could just pull over there and wait..."

"Of course, Ma'am. Anything you wish."

Kim knew that John had 'briefed' all of his employees that Kim was to be given A Plus service. It still embarrassed her a bit. She tried to slip the valet a tip, but he stepped back, acted as if had he taken it, he would have committed a mortal sin.

Kim maneuvered her Yaris into the curbside

passenger loading zone. She turned the engine off and exited her car. The Agent sensed the valet giving her the once over and felt a bit of a thrill. She was wearing a tight-fitting 'cat-suit' that clung to her in all the right places. Kim felt a thrill at obtaining a level of desire from a stranger, knew that she was not correctly acting like a professional Special Agent.

Screw it. Kim was off-duty. If she wanted to use her feminine wiles on the male population, it was her business.

She looked up from the passenger side of her Yaris and saw a familiar face and figure exiting through a secondary exit. Attired in a tight-fitting Asian silk dress with the obligatory slit up the side and a light jacket, Jade walked with a bit of a slink toward the passenger loading zone. She looked up and saw Kim, seemed to hesitate as if about to bolt back inside, but then continued her walk.

Kim called out to her in Mandarin. *"Miss Jade! How are you this evening?"*

Caught now in social congress, Jade's face exhibited a shy smile, then spoke in English.

"Master Wang wishes that I speak as much English as possible. With practice comes skill, he says."

Kim smiled as she approached the young lady. She looked so very young, Kim thought. But her jade eyes had a look of aged experience. She had seen much in her young years.

"Yes. John Wang is correct. And your English is coming along nicely. Do you need a ride? I could—"

"No!" After the Chinese young women spoke, she realized it had come out short and abrasive. She gave a short bow.

"I am sorry. I do not wish to sound... how you

say, not appreciating? But Master Wang has arranged transportation."

Kim stepped closer and gently touched her arm as she replied. "Unappreciative I think is the word you want. And no worries. I should've realized that John would have taken care of your needs."

Jade's smile became less shy.

"Yes," Jade agreed. "He has arranged for me to stay with some older women who work for him. He says it is safer for me, being so young."

"Yes. Young and very pretty. There are those who would take advantage of that."

Jade frowned a bit. "That is true," the young Asian woman said. "But I can't imagine anyone ever taking advantage of you, Mistress Kupar."

Kim winced a little. "Please. Call me, Kim. We are not that much different in age. And, I can tell you have grown up... fast."

Jade looked into Kim's own jade eyes. "You can see that?" she asked.

Kim chuckled. "Yes. My Father gave all us children training and experience in really 'seeing' people as part of running a large business. Then, of course, I became a Special Agent. But I hope I'm not being too nosy or blunt."

Jade's smile became more genuine, less reserved as she replied. "No-Kim. I can see in your own jade colored eyes that you are a caring person, one who is a good friend to many."

"That's a nice compliment, Jade. Thank you." She took the Asian young lady's hand. "And since we share jade colored eyes, would you like to be friends? I know what it's like to be a stranger in a strange land."

"Why yes, Miss... I mean Kim. I would like that!" She clasped Kim's hand in both of hers.

"Here, I have a business card. I'll write my own number on the back." Kim freed her hand and produced a pen and a card from her substantial concealed-carry purse. No way would T-Rex allow her to walk around unarmed, even off duty. Especially after the street attack. She finished writing her number, handed it to Jade.

"Call me anytime," Kim coaxed. "I am a bit of a night-owl."

Jade took the card with some reverence, then bowed low. *"Thank you, kind lady,"* she said in Mandarin. *"I treasure your offer of friendship."*

"Please. No need to bow" urged Kim. *"You're in America now. Friends shake hands or hug here."*

The two jade eyed women clasped hands, began to feel a newfound bond between young persons from different cultures.

A familiar voice rang out in English. "Two of my favorite people becoming acquainted. How lucky am I!"

John Wang strode up, a grin on his face.

"Two visions of loveliness gracing the front of my establishment. If this does not increase my business, I don't know what will."

Kim's mouth formed into a broad smile as she greeted him. "Ever the commensurate politician. Compliments at the drop of a hat."

John closed with Kim, gave her a quick kiss. "I but tell the truth. You are both beautiful. And are among my favorite people."

Jade began to bow. "Master Wang..."

"Please! I overheard what Kim said, and she is

right. Less bowing, more American hugs, and handshakes," John Wang commanded. With that, he reached over and hugged Jade. Kim noticed she returned it, but with a small look of trepidation on her face.

"I was just offering Jade a ride, John," added Kim. "But she said you had it taken care of."

John smiled as he stepped back from the hug. "Yes," he agreed. "In fact, here comes by driver now."

A large man with the look of one of Mongolian descent approached the three, bowed low. *"I am sorry, Master Wang. Stuck in traffic—"* he began in Mandarin.

"Leave earlier." John's smile shut off, then reappeared.

"Yes, Sir."

Jade smiled at Kim, spoke in English. "I hope you have a good evening."

"And you also, Jade. John, please don't work this young lady too hard. She needs to have a life like all other young people."

John's eyebrows raised. "But of course!" he answered. "However, as her mentor, I'm also ensuring she continues with her studies. Her family wants her to go to college."

At the mention of family, Jade stiffened. Kim wondered why.

"Now, young lady, my man here will make sure you have a safe trip home. I will see you tomorrow."

"Yes, Sir," Jade answered and walked off, the Mongolian driver in trail behind.

"She is quite the beauty," said Kim as she watched Jade walk away.

"Yes. And that beauty will attract men who wish

to take advantage of her."

Kim looked at John. "Which is where you come in," said Kim. "As a protective Big Brother."

John smiled and agreed. "Yes, I guess I've taken on the mantle of an older brother. And, do you wish to be an older sister to her?"

"Whatever I can do to help, John," affirmed Kim. "As I told her, I know what it's like to be thrust into a foreign culture and land. Being bounced between three cultures and two very different families made me realize how adapting to new surroundings is not always easy."

John moved in closer, put his arms around her. Kim returned the grasp.

"Ever the helper, the caring person," the Asian business leader whispered in her ear. "Yet you carry a badge and a gun."

Kim smiled and whispered back. "To protect and serve. An old motto that I still take to heart."

John kissed her, and she returned it. Their lips parted, and John murmured in her ear.

"You bring the best out of me, Agent Kupar. You realize that, don't you?"

"I'm flattered," she answered. "However, I don't think you need me to do good, be good."

"Good is not the best, my dear. Come, shall we leave? So that you may have a chance to 'protect and serve'?"

Kim laughed. And it felt good. Whenever she was around John, she laughed a lot. More than she had done in a very long time.

"I think your ideas of protect and serve may be a lot different than what is meant in the traditional sense of the phrase," declared Kim.

"Well, I *was* thinking about a service of breakfast in bed," John admitted. "But a long time after divesting you of you vestments."

Kim nipped his lower lip. "Ever the dog."

"And you nip like a cat. Shall I chase you?" John asked in a low voice.

"No need. Get into my car," the female Agent directed. "Then, to my townhouse."

Now John laughed. "You order me around, as no other."

Kim opened the passenger side door. "Quit complaining," she commanded. "You love it. Now, get in. As T-Rex would say, time's awastin'."

17.

DOWNTOWN STREETS OF SEATTLE

Friday night and Saturday went by way too fast, in Kim's estimation. John had to attend to some 'family business' on Sunday, so Kim caught up on her sleep, then went for a run downtown. Somehow, she wound up, moving toward the Jade Palace. As she realized where she was headed to, Kim thought about a hidden magnetism being the cause.

Love? The word popped into her head, unbidden. She shoved it back. No. Too soon. Right now, she would admit to 'lust,' not 'love,' with all its myriad of complications. So she ran harder, to take her mind out of unwanted territory. Sundays in Downtown Seattle, unless there were special events scheduled, usually meant much fewer people on the streets. So Kim ran smoothly, not having to dodge pedestrians and poor drivers. And today, no rain. Also known as 'liquid sunshine' by the long term natives.

As Kim ran by an alley in the International District, Chinatown to John, she heard a scream emanate from near some garbage dumpsters. She slid to a stop, turned toward the sound. Then another scream. Kim grabbed her Glock 26 compact pistol from her fanny pack, charged in to protect and serve. A young woman stumbled out from behind the dumpsters and sprawled onto the hard concrete of the alleyway. Immediately two Asian males stepped out toward her.

"HALT! Police! Federal Agent!" The words came out in both English and Mandarin automatically. The Asian men looked up at Kim, then saw the gun. One exclaimed in recognized Vietnamese what could only be a curse.

"Hands on head!" Kim ordered as moved just close enough to get a good look at the young female.

"It's that Bitch who hangs around with the Chinaman," one of the Vietnamese males spat out in English.

"Shut up," commanded Kim. "Lady, are you okay?" The woman on the ground began to sob, spoke rapid Vietnamese. Kim knew enough of the language to know she was asking for help, that these two would kill her. Her bloody face added credence to that translation.

Seeing Kim was temporarily distracted by the injured, the two males made a break for it. Kim made an instant decision. The woman was hurt but not dying. And shooting two fleeing what looked like unarmed suspects would start a shit storm. So Kim put on her best sprint.

She had received the Physical Fitness award at FLETC for a reason. The fact she caught up with the slower of the two as he exited the alleyway proved the validity of the medal. Kim sent him sprawling with a soccer-like trip. As the man cried out, his partner turned to look, then accelerated away. Kim came down hard on the glutamate maximus of the miscreant, eliciting a scream of pain. Then the Vietnamese male demonstrated he was not down for the fight. He twisted in some sort of *Kung Fu* type move, kicking and striking at Kim. The battle was on.

He grabbed for her pistol. Kim twisted it from his grasp, then remembered something T-Rex had talked about once.

"A pistol can make a damned fine club if need be. If the Marshal were alive, just ask ole Wyatt Earp about 'buffaloing.'"

So Kim slammed the Glock's square-shaped slide through the man's front teeth. Finger off the trigger of course. He would need some serious dental work, as two top teeth and one bottom were broken off. The young man let out a gurgling scream, grabbed at his mouth. Kim sprang to her feet.

"Want some more, Son of a Bitch?" She spat it out before she knew she was saying it. The man began to choke on his blood and tooth fragments. Kim yanked her cell phone from her fanny pack, hit 911.

"911. Do you have an emergency?"

"Special Agent needs help! Now! One suspect, one victim down. Alleyway near the corner of..."

Like the previous occasion, it seemed like the skies had opened up, rained police and armed federal agents. EMTs soon had the injured woman in an ambulance. One of the Medics, a native Vietnamese, acted as translator.

"They were going to rape her and kill her. She tried to skip out on a human smuggling debt."

"Hers?" Rex asked.

"Sounds like it."

Rex grunted. "Thanks, my friend." He walked over to the back of a SPD patrol car where a none too happy EMT was trying to give the injured suspect first aid.

"Shut up and hold still, dumbass."

The Asian male was far from shutting up. In lisping English through his broken teeth and swollen lips, he cried out. "You tell that bitch we know where she stays, hangs out at!"

T-Rex leaned in past the EMT, inches from the arrestees face.

"That's my partner you're talking about."

The Asian male tried to spit blood through his swollen lips at T-Rex. The EMT magically turned away. Rex grabbed the man's testicles through his loose-fitting pants, crushed and squeezed. The Asian screamed in a high falsetto.

"Hey, I think he needs some pain meds," Rex said for all to hear. "That mouth is really hurting him." The attending EMT tried to keep a straight face, kept failing.

Rex walked over to where Kim was standing. She was talking to a responding patrolwoman, a Detective, and Dennis Spain, the ICE/HSI Duty Agent.

"Yes, I gave chase, caught up with this one. His friend took one look and ran. Then—"

"He attacked you, tried to bite your hand to get the gun," Rex jumped in.

Kim stammered a bit. "Ah, well—"

Dennis caught T-Rex's wink, chimed in.

"That's sure what it looks like. Didn't that happen a lot on the Southwest Border, Rex?"

"Hell yeah! You'd like a thought they were the walking dead, as much as they tried to bite us."

The Detective tried to keep a somber face as he

spoke. "So he was struck in the face as you freed your gun from his grasp."

"Well, yes, I guess—" began Kim.

"Tried to eat another person's gun," continued Rex. "Weird way to commit suicide."

The SPD Patrolwoman lost it, had to turn and walk away. She bent over laughing.

The Detective looked at Rex, then Kim.

"From anybody else, T-Rex, I wouldn't dare report that. From you—" He shook his head, chuckled, closed his notebook and walked away. Kim looked at Rex.

"Is there anybody who does not know you?" she questioned.

Rex shrugged. "Outside of law enforcement, probably."

Kim frowned continued. "Why the- unusual justification for my actions?"

"Mother ICE likes everything to fit into a nice box, wrapped up by a bow of regulations and training manuals," Rex explained. "Slamming a gun slide and barrel through an a-holes teeth is not Standing Operating Procedures, SOP."

"But he was trying to take my pistol—"

Rex shook his head. "There you go again, being logical," he intoned. "Works in the laboratory, not with federal bureaucracy."

An unfortunate familiar voice yelled out in anger.

"Agent Kupar! What trouble are you in now?" It was Group Supervisor Salmon.

"She's in no trouble. She stopped an attempted rape and murder," Rex shot back.

A red-faced Salmon stormed up to the trio of Agents.

"And what are you doing here, Moyer? You're not the Duty Agent, Spain here is."

"He called me as she's my partner and my trainee."

Salmon huffed. "Some trainer you are! She's only been on the job, what, about a year total time and already she's been involved in assaults, shootings—"

"Hey, 'real' Special Agents spend time on the streets, arrest people, stop crimes," interrupted Rex. "Not do high end running shoe fraud cases from behind a desk."

If possible, Salmon's face became redder. "Just because you spent time as a Border Rat, does not make you the superior Agent you think you are," Salmon hissed.

"Better than being a mouse hiding behind a desk," Rex snapped back.

Salmon's eyes bugged out. "I ought to…"

Rex glared at him. "Take your best shot, Shorty…"

"What in Hell are you two doing?" ASAC Tim Weiss' voice cut through the argument.

"Why are you two arguing out here, on the street, in front of public and other law enforcement officers? You think that makes us look professional?"

"Agent Kupar here keeps getting in the middle of things she shouldn't. She—" Salmon glared at Rex and Kim as he tried to continue. Weiss cut him off.

"Oh, I see. Stopping a possible homicide in progress is bad. Having another dead unidentified Asian female is 'good,' right?"

"That's not what I—" Salmon tried to stammer out. Rex grinned at his extreme discomfort.

"And you." Sam now turned his attention on T-Rex. "This 'I'm old; therefore I know everything' is *getting* old. There are supervisors for a plethora of reasons. One reason is to keep you in line."

"Boss," Rex began a reply.

Tim cut him off as he had Salmon.

"Don't 'boss' me. Quit being such a stubborn pain in my rear." He now looked and spoke at Kim. "You okay? You've had more action in a month than many Agents have in a career."

"Yes, Sir. I am fine."

Sam stuck his hand out. "Good work, good reactions. If you have any problems with OPR, let me know. Saving women from rape and death makes Homeland Security look good, not to mention it's the right thing to do."

The ASAC looked at Rex and Salmon. "Okay. This is over," he declared. "Salmon, make sure this young lady gets anything she needs to write a report on this incident. And Moyer, you make sure she gets home okay, in the Office on Monday."

"Yes, Sir. I'll make sure she gets turned over to Matt Monday—"

"Who said anything about Matt Swenson as her Training Agent?" Weiss asked. "Congratulations. You get to work for a living until you retire. Maybe it will help with your hard-headed attitude if you're kept busy."

Sam looked up at the detectives from SPD. "Now get to work, while I go schmooze a bit."

Salmon stomped off, his face still red. Kim looked at a now non-smiling Rex.

"Sorry if I'm causing you more work."

Rex waved her off. "Water off a ducks back. Sam

is probably right. Working with you keeps me from sitting around the office, bitching." Rex paused, then glanced at ASAC Weiss, talking to the SPD personnel.

"Come on. Let's get while the getting is good," Rex directed.

"Just a minute," interjected Kim. "I want to check on the victim." Kim walked over to the ambulance containing the beat up young woman. The young lady, probably not yet twenty years of age, looked up as Kim approached, began to point and ramble in Vietnamese.

"Please, Ma'am. My Vietnamese is limited. Do you speak English at all?"

The woman reached out and grabbed Kim's hand, held it to her breast. "Thank You!" Then she began to sob. Kim reached in and hugged her. She looked at the Vietnamese speaking EMT.

"You have her name?"

"Her given, our first name, is *Bich*," replied the EMT. "Translates as Jade or Gemstone."

Kim looked at her tear filled eyes. Jade. They were jade in color. Like hers and another young lady Kim knew. What was the possibility of three women from three different cultures, all with jade eyes, coming into contact in this city, mused Kim. The Special Agent pointed at her eyes.

"We have something in common. Jade eyes."

The EMT translated what Kim had said, and Bich's eyes widened. She rattled something off in her native language, which the EMT translated for Kim.

"She said you were fated to meet. That God smiled on you both."

Kim smiled as she answered. "I hope she's right. Here, I have my card... Please explain that she can call me anytime. I'll work on obtaining a parole into the U.S. for her as a Sex Trafficking victim."

After the EMT translated this, the young Vietnamese woman smiled again, grasped Kim's hand and said, "Friend.".

"Sister," Kim replied. Later, Kim would wonder why she referred to her as 'sister'. At that moment, however, it felt right.

Kim turned and walked back to Rex.

"New friend?" Rex asked.

"Yes, I think so," Kim replied. "Now, if I can have that ride back to my place. I am suddenly becoming rather tired."

"Your wish is my command."

"Well, if that is the case, how about you clean my townhouse today," suggested Kim

"Don't push your luck, young lady. Just remember a T-Rex is still above a Raptor on the food chain, as the apex predator," the Senior Agent informed Kim.

Kim smiled and sassed a bit. "Even old and long in the tooth T-Rexes?"

"Respect your elders. Come on. I have an irritated wife waiting at home. This disrupted our plans."

Kim gave Rex a sideways glance as she spoke. "Like you said, no rest for the wicked."

"Just have to keep pushing, Kim," Rex warned. "Just have to keep pushing."

18.

TOWNHOUSE, DOWNTOWN SEATTLE

K im invited Rex up to see her place, but he begged off.
"Like I said, my wife has plans for me. I need to get home. Call me if anyone bothers you, including Salmon."

Kim smiled. Ever a protective Dutch Uncle.

"Yes. Sir," she replied

"And drop the 'sir'. Again that was my father."

As he turned away to leave, Kim patted his arm.

"Thanks for being there," she said.

Rex grunted. "Like I said, I take the role of Training Agent serious. And now you're stuck with me."

"Could be worse, Rex," declared Kim. "At least things have not been dull."

The Senior Special Agent guffawed, then answered. "Understatement of the year. See you tomorrow."

As Rex walked to the elevator, Kim heard her

personal cell phone ring. She shut the door, looked at the number of the called, and smiled.

"*Hello. John,*" she said in Mandarin.

"*Are you okay?*" John exclaimed. "*I just heard what happened. The Asian community is abuzz about you saving a young Vietnamese girl.*"

Kim laughed. "*Your intelligence system strikes again. The government could take some guidance from you on how to keep on top of things,*" she observed.

"*Well, I would not be a good steward of the Asian businesses as their President if I didn't know of the problems in our area,*" he opined. "*And I guess Vietnamese gangs are still a problem.*"

"*So you have dealt with them before?*" Kim asked.

John sighed over the phone. "*Yes, unfortunately. Much like the Tongs, the Triad, and the Yakuza, they are like weeds that grow through cracks in the sidewalk. They never seem to disappear completely, are always popping up in my China Town.*"

"*Well, it seems they're running a human trafficking operation now,*" stated the female Agent.

"*That is not what is important to me. Kim. The question is, are you all right?*"

Kim smiled into the cellphone as she answered. "*Yes, I am. My training helped keep me safe.*"

"*Then I will have to thank T-Rex, as he is your Trainer. For, my jade beauty, the thought of you being hurt or out of my life—*" John Wang let the end of the sentence hang, concern in his voice evident even over the phone. Kim felt an odd feeling in her stomach.

"*Are you... free to come over?*"

"*Yes, Kim,*" John answered without hesitation. "*Any more business can wait. As the expression goes, I'll be there soon with bells on."*

Kim smiled and replied. *"Well, then, I may just have to remove those bells—"*

19.

Kim was in the office early, banging out her report about the incident with the Vietnamese gang members. As she worked, Rex glanced at her Report of Investigation (ROI in office speak) and kvetched on how she described what had occurred.

"You responded to the cries for help, identifying yourself as a Federal Agent and Law Enforcement Officer."

"That is what I said, Rex."

"No, you said it differently," he informed her. "Trust ole T-Rex. Certain verbiage satisfies the Courts and OPR."

"Oh, all right. Anything to keep my 'Dutch uncle' off my back. Or, are you my second mother?" Kim sassed back.

"Just because I have a belly does not mean I'm pregnant or can give birth, Raptor," Rex announced.

Kim grinned at T-Rex. Funny how that nickname was growing on her. At last, when Rex used it.

Matt Swenson stuck his head into their cubicle, this being his first full day back at work.

"Save that report in the computer. Kim. Rex, you and her, into the conference room. Things are changing fast." Then he was gone. Rex frowned.

"Hurry up meeting on Monday morning. Not good," he declared

"Am I in trouble over what happened?" Fretted Kim.

"No, Kim," Rex assured. "They would've called you into the ASAC office. This is something else."

Kim saved the report, turned off her computer. Cyber Security was a must in this day of hacking of government and personal files.

Kim and Rex went to the conference room and found ASAC Weiss, Supervisor Salmon, as well as Anne Knutsen, the Group Supervisor for the Human Trafficking group. With her were two of her Agents, Jim Munson and Ly Tran, a Vietnamese of former refugee status.

The ASAC quickly came to the point.

"We are setting up our Title III room for a wiretap operation. Kim, you and Rex's activities have uncovered an extensive human trafficking operation in our own backyard of which we had no clue. Thanks to some follow-up on that shipping container case and some paperwork the malcontent you took out in the alley had on him, we have a direct business tie in we can target."

"What is that, Boss?" Rex asked.

"Madam Chou's Massage Parlor, in the International District. You know it?"

Rex smiled and acknowledged. "Yeah, by reputation only. If my Better Half caught me getting a massage, I'd be singing soprano."

This elicited some light laughter from the others in the room.

ASAC Weiss continued. "Well, Matt Swenson has started the criminal complaint and official request for a Title III Court Order. We should have the Federal District Judges court order in the next couple of days. Then all we have to do is have our Technical Agent get the targeted telephone taps up and running. We may develop some Internet feed from this also. Thus, Matt here's Cybercrimes expertise. "

Tom Weis looked directly at Kim as he spoke. "We also need your Mandarin skills. Along with Ly Tran's native Vietnamese. We have a request out for TDY Asian language speakers also, with D.C. footing the bill."

"This sounds big," Group Supervisor Anne Knutsen said, frowning. A native of Puget Sound, she had managed to stay in Seattle for her entire career. Plus she was a native Norwegian speaker.

"Yes. Anne," the ASAC replied. "The attack on Kim here, and then her saving that Vietnamese woman drew the attention of the National Press and Headquarters. We are expected to get to the bottom of this human smuggling ring ASAP. So, your Group will be the one heading up this investigation, with Matt, Kim and Rex temporarily assigned to you. This type of crime is your bailiwick, but these three have specific skill sets helpful for this investigation."

"Of course." She smiled at Kim. "Welcome aboard," greeted Anne.

"Thank you," Kim replied. Things were moving so fast. It was hard to believe that just last year she was still in FLETC.

"Okay. You all have your marching orders," Weiss

declared. "And to answer your unasked question, Rex, you are still Kim's official training Agent. So, keep up on the training reports."

"Yeah, Boss. No rest for the wicked."

Weiss laughed. "You got that right. Okay, take off. A lot needs to be done fast. As in Yesterday."

20.

TOWNHOUSE, DOWNTOWN SEATTLE

It was almost 10.00 PM before Kim made it back to her townhouse. She walked in and plunked down onto her stuffed sofa. For the first time, she began to feel older than her some thirty years of age. The last couple of days had been exhausting and stressful, even with her 'stress relief' activities with John. The thought brought a smile to her lips.

Her cell phone rang. She pulled it out of her pocket and looked at the number. It was her younger brother, A.J.eet.

"Hey. A.J. what's up."

"Hey, Sis. You got a few minutes?" he asked. "I'd like to talk to you about something. Can I come by?"

Kim sighed, then replied. "Yes, but just for a little while. I just got home, have to hit the ground running in the morning."

"Busy, huh?"

"Understatement of the year," state Kim. "Come on over. But be quick. I need a shower and a soft bed".

Ten minutes later and Kim was letting A.J. into her place. She was in a kimono style robe with her black hair down. It felt good to relax like a normal young lady. She hugged A.J., handed him a cold beer.

"Here, hate to drink alone," she advised.

"Yeah, Kim. I know the feeling," agreed A.J.

They moved to the sofa. Kim sat and tucked her legs up under her as she sipped her beer.

"So, little brother, what's up?"

A.J. paused for a moment as if contemplating his beer. Then, he said, "I'm getting closer to Jade. We have coffee after work sometimes, though she still is hesitant about an actual 'date.'

Kim examined her brother. A.J. was usually the happy go lucky, easy going one of the siblings. This night, he seemed on edge.

"And this is a problem, A.J.?" Questioned Kim. "Is John Wang involved, upset about Jade spending time with you?"

"Not that I know of," he answered. "Jade does seem a little afraid of his-displeasure, I guess would be the right term. But I'm certain he knows we talk, see each other. You know he has eyes and ears everywhere."

Kim smiled and agreed. "Yes. He is building a mini-empire as the President of the Seattle Asian Business Association. But he seems genuinely interested in bettering the lot for everyone."

"I know, Sis. I don't think this involves him," her brother stated. "But it does involve some things I have seen, heard."

"Well, spit it out, A.J.," Kim directed her brother. "You were never one to hold back your opinions as a child, not to anyone."

A.J. finally grinned. "Yeah, I used to really p*ss off, Father," he said. "He thought I was way too opinionated to the point of being disrespectful to my elders." He paused, then continued sans grin. "I was out walking the other day and saw Jade come out of Madam Chou's."

"So?"

"Oh come, one Sis," A.J. chided his sister. "It's all over China Town. Madam Chou's is famous, or infamous, for 'happy endings' in her massage business. Everyone knows she runs prostitutes through her business. I'm surprised that Seattle Vice has not closed her down."

Kim paused for a moment. She had to be careful; she did not let on that ICE was suddenly interested in the Madam.

"Knowing something and being able to prove it in court is often two separate things," Kim stated. "So, exactly how is this involving Jade?"

"Well, she saw me down the street, seemed to turn as if to run the other direction. I called out and walked up to her." He paused, then continued.

"She was scared."

"About what?" Questioned Kim.

"She never said," A.J. replied. "She just quickly told me that she was dropping off something for Mr. Wang. I told her, hey, no big deal, did she have a moment for coffee. Just then, one of Wang's limos pulled up, and Jade said she had to leave. Almost ran to the limo. That big Mongolian guy got out, looked at me, had Jade get in the back seat, then grinned at me."

"Well, so?" Kim queried him again. "At least he didn't start yelling at you and Jade—"

"It was the most scary, almost evil grin I have

seen outside a horror flick!" A.J. blurted out, his face now flushed.

Kim frowned, leaned forward. She saw that A.J. was very upset, entirely out of character for him. She put her hand on his knee.

"Hey, Little Brother. This really has you worked up, doesn't it?" Kim asked.

"Yeah, Kim, it does," he agreed. "First time in a long time that I get this... feeling like something bad is about to happen. But I don't know what." He stared into Kim's eyes as he spoke.

"Remember when you told me how it was when that Tiger was stalking you and Uncle? That you knew that danger had targeted you?"

Kim looked deeper into her brother's eyes. He was frightened to the bone.

"Yes," she said. "And I can see that you are scared for Jade-right?"

A.J. nodded his head 'yes.'

Kim moved closer, put her arm around A.J.'s shoulders. "Think because you have strong feelings for her that you are getting overly protective?"

A.J.'s mouth formed a slight grin as he answered. "Yeah. I thought of that. But-I just can't shake that feeling of some-nasty force is stalking Jade."

Kim gave her younger brother a quick peck on his cheek.

"Tell you what. Ole bossy sister will do some snooping around, unofficial now so don't get any ideas. If I think there is anything that may be a threat to you and Jade, I'll let you know. Then, it might become official."

"You're not going to let John Wang know—" began A.J.

"That you talked to me? Please! I'm a trained Federal Agent," Kim declared. "I think I can obtain a little info from him if need be, without him getting suspicious."

A.J. produced a sly grin. "Pillow talk, you mean?" he asked.

Kim's mouth popped open. She grabbed A.J. in a headlock. "Just remember your Big Sister can STILL kick your ass!" she scolded.

A.J. managed to wriggle free, then returned the favor and used his knuckles to give her a "nuggey" on her head. Kim squealed, poked him in the ribs. A.J. let go and jumped up, ran behind the sofa. Kim bounded over the back and began to chase him around her townhouse.

"When I catch you-!"

It was if they had never grown up, were still children playing games in a world that was often too serious.

It felt good.

21.

WIRE ROOM, ICE/HSI
OFFICE OF THE SPECIAL AGENT IN CHARGE
SEATTLE, WASHINGTON

Four days later and Kim was sitting in the Seattle SAC/HSI "Wire Room". The specially designed electronic surveillance site had been set up years prior and had been the location of many a successful Federal wiretap. Now, of course, there were many more cell phone towers and other areas of electronic communications that were surreptitiously surveilled rather than the traditional 'wire' phone lines.

Kim was handling the listening post along with Ly Trang, the former South Vietnamese refugee turned Federal Agent. So far, Madam Chou's telephone lines had been the source of conversations in Mandarin, Vietnamese, English, as well as a little Korean and Japanese. Kim knew enough Korean and Japanese to catch at least the gist of the conversation to determine relevance. Contrary to the 'Hollywood Version,' law enforcement did not tap and tape everything spoken over the surveilled communications devices. Only conversations involving possible connections to the alleged criminal activity were listened to and recorded. After the first fifteen seconds or so, if the conversation was clearly about some mundane items, they stopped listening. They would monitor about every half to full minute to see if the conversation remained non-controversial. Everything was translated and transcribed by either National Guard personnel or contract personnel with the required security clearances. There just were not enough Special Agents to do everything. Title III Wiretap Investigations were time and staff intensive.

Ly Trang was listening to a Vietnamese conversation between one of the 'massage girls' and a regular client. The young lady was trying to fit the man into her schedule as he was trying to smooth talk her into an outside date. Ly swore in disgust. Then he mumbled in accented English "God Damn Communists!" The telephone conversation ended, and Ly cut his earphones. He noticed Kim had a quizzical look on her face.

"North Vietnamese man. North and South have different accents, way of talking. I can tell."

"And thus you call the North Vietnamese speakers Communists?" Kim asked.

"Yes!" Ly snarled. "The Northern dogs invaded us, took over our country, and stole everything. My family hid in the hills. I was born in the hills. A few years later, my father was caught, sent to a re-education camp, which was a prison. Because he had worked with the Americans, he was a traitor to *Ho Chi Min.*"

Ly spat bile into the trash can. "Everything of value was taken by the Communists. Half my family fled, then emigrated to here. Then those Communist dogs come over here, to make money! Lying sacks of shit! I see them, hear them speak in stores, I tell them to go back to their communist masters. They do not belong in this free country."

Ly stopped, took a deep breath. "Sorry. I just get mad sometimes."

"Your father survived?" Kim asked.

"Yes. Barely," Ly answered. "Ten years in prison. Then allowed to leave. Along with my two sisters. My mother and aunts are still trying to come here. It is a big game for the Communists. They make us beg to leave to show their power."

Kim patted his arm as she reassured him. "Just know that I and others appreciate you. You're a good Agent and American, Ly. I'm glad you're here."

The Vietnamese Agent smiled. "Thank You," Ly relied. "Sorry I am so-grumpy."

"You're like me, Ly. You hate injustice. It makes us all 'grumpy.'"

"How's the equipment working?" Kelly Olivet stuck his head around the corner of the extended counter area where the listening stations were set. Kelly was the Technical Agent extraordinaire who had set the entire Title Three room up years ago, was still in Seattle. His expertise was legendary in ICE. He was often sent TDY to help other offices with technical problems. In addition to the 'Wire Room,' Kelly kept all the surreptitious recording and camera equipment up and operating, to include the surveillance vans and wiring up Undercover Agents for undercover meets.

"Just fine, Kelly," answered Kim. "Sound quality is good on the hard line as well as the cell phones."

"Good," he said. "Aim to please. Can I get you two some coffee?"

"Tea for me. Ly?"

"Tea also. Thanks."

Kelly chuckled. "All my years in Chicago as a Cop, no one drank tea, we were all coffee junkies," he mused. "I come to the land of Starbucks, and half you people start drinking tea."

Kim laughed. She liked Kelly's sense of humor, his positive support of all LEOs he worked with. She could imagine he was a 'Good Cop' in Chicago. Kim also wondered why he had never married. In her eyes, he would have been a right candidate for many women. Even now aging, he would make a decent partner for someone.

"Well, Asia is still tea land, Kelly. Despite being invaded by Starbucks."

"Ain't that the truth," Kelly declared. "Be right back with the tea."

"Thanks, Kelly," Ly chimed in.

As Kelly left, the computer screen set up to cover Tweets and Text messages sprang to life.

Ly glanced at it. "Mandarin. Bet you it is the 'Boss' again."

This first full day of wiretapping had resulted in a shadowy figure who was known as the Boss communicated only through tweeting, texting, and e-mails. Kelly and Matt were trying to pin down the Boss's server or modem, but so far the person had developed some means of changing both his cellphone and electronic communications equipment on what was at least a daily basis, sometimes more often. Whomever the Boss was, he was experienced in dealing with the realities of potential electronic eavesdropping and surveillance.

As Kim read the text coming over the tapped lines, the encrypted radios crackled into existence. T-Rex's familiar voice came over the speaker.

"Alpa-16 here. You have activity at your end, Raptor?"

Kim winced. Typical Rex. Non-standard old school radio speak and using her new nickname like a C.B. radio handle.

"Alpha-16, Base here has text activity. Are you seeing something there?" Kim asked in reply.

Rex Moyer was in charge of this days Mobile Surveillance Team, had some four other Agents in G-Rides out with him, spread out around the streets near Madam Chou's. Other than some businessmen as well as typical ne'er-do-wells, probably trying to get a 'quickie' or a Happy Ending, there had been nothing of any import.

"We have the woman in charge out front texting like mad. She does not look happy, from my Eyeball position," Rex advised.

'Eyeball' was the forward surveillance unit with the primary line of sight on the targets.

Kim scanned the texting as fast as she could. The communicators were using a kind of 'pidgin' Mandarin to in their texting, so she had a double difficulty in translating to English. She frowned.

"Alpha-16, something involving-sickness or injury is happening inside—Oh, God. I think someone died!" Kim called out.

"How? Specifics, Agent," Rex shot back. Kim scanned, her brain working a mile a minute.

"I think a- 'working girl' was attacked. Stand by."

"Times a wasting if someone is dying, Raptor."

Kim's face flushed in concentration.

"The woman is texting-a customer is down also. Something bad is happening. The Boss is texting her back that he will send someone to clean up her mess."

"That the same Boss from the other day?" Rex inquired.

"Affirmative—Alpha-16, watch for men in a vehicle arriving, either in front or the alley. This is going to happen fast," warned Kim.

"Roger That." Then Rex was all business, arranging his surveillance units to ensure any vehicle coming and leaving would be tailed. Kim sat on the edge of her chair, the texting had stopped.

Five minutes later, Rex called out on the radio.

"We have a black Limo in front of the location. Two Asian men jumping out met an agitated boss woman. Now, they are inside."

The action paused for a few minutes. Then, Rex again. "Hot damn, they are carrying out a rolled up rug out the front door! I don't believe they are doing this in broad daylight. All surveillance units be prepared to move."

The four units all acknowledged. Then Rex again. "All right. On the move—"

Ly and Kim stayed fixed to the radio speaker as Rex coordinated the 'tail' of the limo. Kim could tell just how experienced Rex was as he smoothly ordered the units around, called out the locations of the target vehicle, and coordinated the swapping of the 'Eyeball' so as not to tip the target vehicle off to the surveillance.

"Alright, be advised, the limo is pulling next to an old warehouse on South Washington Street, down by the area of the Big Bertha Tunnel," Rex advised. "I thought some of these buildings had been closed due to the tunnel project."

"Address, Rex," requested Kim.

Rex read off the address, and Kim quickly used the Homeland Security Computer System to search for and obtain ownership records.

"Owned by Red Sun Import Export Corporation. Looks like a recently formed company."

"Ten-Four," Rex acknowledged. "The two Asians just took the rug out of the limo, and are carrying it into the back of the warehouse. Surveillance Team, get ready for an Exigent Circumstances Entry. Looks like some blood dripping from the rug."

"Belay that order." It was ASAC Weiss cutting into the net. "I've got Matt standing by run up a Search Warrant to the Federal Magistrate."

"But, Boss. Someone might be dying in there!" Rex protested loudly over the radio.

"My call. I guarantee they are already dead. Snakeheads don't want live witnesses to their operations when they go bad."

There radio was silent. Kim thought she could have cut the silence with a knife. Then Rex spoke.

"Okay, Boss. We'll set up a perimeter. Do we stop anybody from leaving?"

"Find an excuse to stop them with the marked SPD Unit you have standing by," directed Weiss. "Matt's been following this, has a template set up for a Warrant. He'll have it to the judge shortly."

Kim knew that T-Rex was chomping at the bit. If it were anybody but Tim Weiss that had broken in, the Senior Agent might have claimed 'radio problems' and busted in. But he had too much respect for the ASAC to put him in a trick bag.

22.

The ASAC had been right about Matt Swenson's abilities to obtain a formal warrant. A half hour later, Matt literally ran it to U.S. Magistrate and had it quickly signed. Then he drove it to the waiting Rex with additional Agents in tow. Kim listened in frustration as she heard the Units line up and hit the warehouse with battering ram and ballistic shield. Rex had been one of the Senior Trainers whom had ensured everyone was trained and practiced in the most current ICE certified entry tactics.

"Damn, I want to be there," Kim said to herself.

"You and me both. Kim" agreed Ly Tran.

Within ten minutes, Rex reported two in custody, no shooting, no injuries. And, ASAC Weiss had been correct. Two dead bodies, client and sex worker, were found wrapped in the rug.

"We need a Mandarin speaker here," called out Rex over the radio. "They no speakie the English."

"On my way," Kim radioed back. She set a near

land speed record driving from the SAC Office to the scene. She parked her Mustang and leaped out. Rex was standing by a marked SPD Unit, two Asian males handcuffed and leaning against the vehicle, one front, one back.

"Kept them on ice, separated for you, Kim," said Rex.

"Thanks, Rex." Kim stepped up and froze. The one leaning against the front of the police cruiser she knew as one of John Wang's drivers. She did not know his name but had seem him at the Jade Palace.

"Have an I. D., on him, Rex?" she asked.

"Yeah, but I bet you it's fake. Sammy Wong. Yeah, right," replied Rex.

"Limo registration?"

"To the Red Star Import Export Corporation you found," came the reply.

Kim paused, took a deep breath, and let it out.

"Well, here goes."

Kim walked up to the alleged Mr. Wong. As soon as he saw her, he smiled, spoke in Mandarin.

"*John Wang's whore. Now I know I am not in trouble.*"

"*And why is that, my rude friend?*" Kim shot back in kind.

"*If you have not figured that out, then you're as stupid as you are good looking. Too bad I didn't see you first,*" the Chinese driver sneered.

"*So, Mr. Wang knows of your... additional activities besides driving?*"

The smile on the good sized Chinese male turned into a smirk.

"*I want a lawyer, Whore.*"

"That won't do you any good. See you in prison."

Rex walked up to her side. "He just insult you?"

"Yes," replied Kim. "Then he lawyered up."

"Want him to have the scenic, bumpy view to the lockup?" Rex asked.

Kim looked at him as she replied. "Being called names by the likes of him means nothing to me. He was found with two dead bodies. He won't not see the so-called light of day for a long while."

Kim approached the other man, a supposed Charles Chan (really?), who lawyered up immediately. She was about to start looking at some Chinese language paperwork that had been found when Dennis Spain, part of the Search Team, walked up to her.

"Kim, we found something weird I'd like you to look at."

"What is it?" Kim asked.

"It'll be easier to show you than explain," Dennis said.

Kim followed Dennis into the downtown warehouse. Someone had found the main light switch and the larger overhead lights illuminated the entire warehouse floor.

In the far corner was a large barred cage, similar to the one discovered in the shipping Conex with the two dead women and dead Panda. Kim slowly walked up and crouched down near the open cage door.

"Is that what I think it is," Dennis asked as he pointed to a clump of something hanging on the edge of the door.

Kim used her plastic-gloved hands to remove the clump of what could only be thick strands of fur.

"Well, I'll be whipped. Large feline hair." She

looked at it closely, sniffed it. "Bet you it's the same as that Bengal Tiger based sample from the container cage," she said to Dennis.

Dennis smiled. "Thought this would give you a thrill," he declared.

Kim gingerly placed it into a paper evidence bag. "It smells damp," Kim stated. "A very big cat was here not long ago." She stood up. "Now the question is, where did it go?"

23.

A SPD SWAT Team backed by the VICE Squad and some ICE Agents hit Madam Chou's within minutes of the warehouse raid. A surveillance van had kept an eye on the place while Rex and company had followed the limousine to the warehouse. Kim missed the sight of screaming and yelling 'massage therapists' and the 'Johns' being rounded up and placed in various transport vans. One person not put in for transport with the others was Madam Chou.

Kim walked up to the caged patrol vehicle Madam Chou was sitting in. Her face reflected the stereotypical Asian stoicism as she looked at her previous business establishment.

"*Madam Chou,*" Kim spoke in Mandarin to the middle-aged but still attractive Chinese woman. The woman looked at Kim, smirked a bit.

"*You know I will want a lawyer. So, John Wang's friend, you're wasting your time talking with me.*"

"*I guess everyone in the International District*

knows me then. Why is that?" Questioned Kim.

Madam Chou frowned. *"You really do not know the position you are in, do you?"* she said.

Kim paused for a moment, trying to read something into the Madam's body language.

"I am supposed to know something, Madam Chou?" Kim asked.

The Madam kept frowning as she spoke. *"Young Lady, take it from one who knows. John Wang is not someone you should associate with. You may have a target on your back."*

"Why? Because he is the President of the Asian Business Association?"

The Chinese woman barked out a laugh, sneered. *"You need to do some homework-by yourself."*

Kim harrumphed. *"You're speaking in riddles. If you know something, tell me. You are facing serious charges for your involvement with two deaths. I could talk to the U.S. Attorney, see about reduced charges—"*

The Madam laughed again. *"Then I would be a meal for Sir Kahn!"* she loudly declared.

"Who? Look, I can offer witness protection—"

"I've said too much already!" The Madam blurted out. *"Your youth and innocence seems to bring the mothering instinct out in me, makes me want to talk. Now, it's time for me to shut my mouth. I want a lawyer!"*

Kim looked at the Madam as the Chinese woman stared straight ahead. She turned and walked over to Dennis Spain, who was talking to Seattle Vice Squad Members.

"I tried, Dennis. She clammed up."

"Yeah, we figured she would, but we had to try," Dennis said.

"Anybody ever hear of a Sir Khan?" Asked Kim.

The Vice Officers and Dennis shook their heads. "The madam mention him-or her?" Asked Dennis.

"Yes. And Chou is afraid of that name. So... wait a minute," said Kim.

Kim walked over to her vehicle. Took the evidence bag with the fur sample in it and walked back to Madam Chou. With a gloved hand, she removed the sample and held it in front of the Madam's field of vision. The Asian woman's eyes widened, and she cried out. *"Get away from me! GET AWAY FROM ME!"* She began to cry and sob as she tried to lean against her seat belt away from Kim.

The Special Agent walked back to a quizzical Dennis. "What is she, a Vampire and you showed her garlic-or a cross?"

"No," Kim answered. "A fur sample I am about to take to Woodland Park Zoo, for some help in identification. See you back in the office with Rex."

"You be careful, Kim. Sounds as if you have something that some people are terrified of," advised Kim's fellow Agent.

"Yes. And I need to know why."

24.

WOODLAND PARK ZOO, SEATTLE

K im loved the smell of the Big Cat House, officially now called the Large Feline Exhibit and Sanctuary. It always brought back fond memories of her time here as a grad student and researcher on her original path of being a Zoologist. Funny, she thought, how her first contact with a Big Cat had been in helping to kill one, yet now she still had a love affair with the large predators. Then she saw the person whom the word 'love' had been associated with her in the not so distant past. Before John Wang. Hank Thomas saw her approach and walked toward her, grinning as he greeted her.

"Twice in two weeks, my favorite Tiger Lady comes around. Someone upstairs must like me."

Kim smiled, memories of the good feelings of the past pushing up from some partially hidden recess of her brain. These thoughts made her feel at odds with the world as she greeted Hank.

"Not like, Hank. As I have an unpleasant riddle to

work on with your help."

Hank gave her a quick one-armed hug. "So, what do you have? It must be more than just a simple riddle for you to come back here."

"Here." Kim showed Hank the new fur sample. The Zoologist and large animal keeper frowned.

"This is fresh. You have the cat it belongs to?" he queried.

"I think I just missed it," Kim answered

"How so?"

"Well, it's like this—"

Kim gave him a quick and dirty rundown of the day's two search warrants.

"Now, this is all secret, official business between you and me."

Hank made the motions of zipping his mouth shut. "Lips are sealed. You said that woman went nuts when showed this sample?"

"Yes," explained the Special Agent. "Mentioned a 'Sir Kahn', something about being eaten."

Hank paused, deep in thoughts. Then he responded.

"Name is very close to the Tiger in Kipling's 'The Jungle Book'. Various films made based on the book over the years. Never ran across it while in India?"

"I never read much Kipling, though I know he has a special place in Indian history," answered Kim. "But ignoring the source behind the name, how in all that is holy do you move a huge tiger around in broad daylight? In and around downtown Seattle? Even sedated, just the size of the cage to hold it would attract attention. And, where do you keep it on a day-by-day basis? Bengal's can be a noisy handful."

"Well, since you said this involves a criminal organization, they must have the manpower and sufficient discreet locations to hide a large cat," opined Hank. "If they can move bunches of smuggled people, then they must have figured out how to move a Bengal."

Kim paused on thought, then shook her head as she spoke. "People of Asian descent moving around the International District could easily be ignored. But a tiger? Or a large cage? Man, you'd have to have some power to keep people from talking."

"Hell, Kim. Think about it," declared Hank. "If you knew you'd be eaten by a huge predator, wouldn't *you* keep your yap shut about such matters? Not to mention the historical tendencies of Chinese and other Asians to keep their problems in house, away from us 'barbarians.'"

Kim sighed. "Yeah, you're right," Kim agreed. "I just keep hoping that the nice people I met in traditional China Town would be more cooperative."

Hank smiled as he answered. "Ever the optimist. I take it you want me to do a complete work-up on this new sample, compare it to the others for genetic similarities?"

"Yes, Please. I'd owe you big time," Kim informed Hank.

"De nada, as they say. Anything for my favorite Tiger Lady."

Hank was one of the very few people, now Rex included, whom Kim had confided in about her 'Bengal Tiger Hunt.' Zoo personnel especially might not take kindly to someone who killed a member of an endangered species. Kim smiled, reached out, and grabbed his hand as she talked.

"Thanks, my excellent friend. If I can do anything in return—"

"There is one thing, Kim."

"What's that, Hank?" she asked

The large and buff man took a deep breath, let it out. Then he spoke.

"I want you to accept my apology."

Kim's mouth popped open in surprise.

"For what? Hank, you have me completely confused!" she exclaimed.

"When you said you were leaving the Zoo, and me, for a new career, I was... really nasty," apologized the muscular Zoologist.

Kim had put the memory of that day into the deepest recesses of her mind. It had hurt. But now-

"Hank, look it," Kim began. "What is done is done. But since you brought it up, I never said I was leaving YOU. That was what you said."

Suddenly, an unexpected, frustration boiled over. First, high-pressure investigation in a new group. Then, a new lover. Next, not only being called a Whore but being told that her new significant other was a source of possible danger and disruption. And now, this! Old wounds re-opened. And for what ends?

"God Dammit Hank!" she suddenly yelled. "I do NOT need this right now. We already had this conversation a while ago. Like I said, you said I was leaving you, when I wasn't! I just had a chance at a new job, career. NOT, a complete new life. There is a difference. But no. YOU had to start yelling, making accusations...."

The tears came. Kim did not want them, but they came anyway. Crying with a badge and a gun could look weak to some. She felt she could not allow that.

But her emotions began to dictate what was to happen, not her intellect.

"Dammit! Now, look. I'm crying!" Kim blurted out. "Like some little bitch who can't hack the pressures of my job. It's your fault! Why can't you let things just lie?? Huh? *Why not?!*"

She slapped his muscular chest, hard. Hank hardly moved.

"You and your damned Hulk muscles. Typical over built male. Think you can just, ah ah bully women with your size and strength. Well, let me tell you, you big dumb ox!"

Kim began to sputter, almost incoherent.

"Fuck!" She spun on her heels, stormed out of the Big Cat area.

Moments later, she was sitting on a zoo bench, trying to control her tears. All these months of adapting to the traditional masculine world of Federal Law Enforcement, putting up with the constant examinations of whether she was good enough, and 'tough' enough for this line of work, and now a past love causes her to melt down. Thank God, no one from the office saw this.

"Kim." The voice came from behind her. It was Hank.

"Go away," she ordered.

"I can't just go away. I was trying to apologize for being the a-hole back then. I... I still love you."

"That is supposed to fix everything?" Kim blurted out, then regretted it.

Hank sighed, then said. "No. I know I tried to force you into a box. When you and your partner Rex showed up the other day, I was so glad that you seemed happy. And I realized that if I had not been such a jerk, maybe I would have been part of that happiness. I was selfish, tried to demand that you stay just the way I wanted. I could have followed you if you were stationed out of the area. But... I guess my ego got in the way. Sorry."

Kim half turned toward him. "You know there is someone else," she stated.

"I know. Word gets around. That does not stop me from caring about you. I'll go now. I'll send you a text when I finish the examination of that sample."

Hank turned and started to walk away.

"Oh... Shit!" Kim stood up, faced his direction, and spoke. "You know, you just gave one of the longest speeches about something other than large cats or other zoo animals since I first met you."

Hank stopped, turned, and faced her. "Had lots of time to think about it," he answered. "Maybe I over thought it. Again, sorry."

"If you say sorry one more time-!" Kim warned.

"You'll kick my ass," was his reply.

Kim started to sputter, then closed the distance, grabbed his shirt collar. Memories flooded in again with his comment harkened back to many a playful tussle. She pulled his face down to her eye level, tried to stay angry, but could not.

"Okay!" she blurted. "You win. I accept your apology. I, I... oh Hell, right now I don't know what I want."

Hank gently stroked her cheek with his fingers as he asked, "Want to talk about it?"

Kim slowly pushed him back. "I can't. It involves... work. So I can't share the details with you."

Hank stood, back straight, looked at Kim as he said, "Just remember, I'm always here for you."

"Which is not fair to you, Hank." Kim looked into her former love's (was it really 'former'?) eyes. "You just made me realize how much I care for you... again!" she declared.

"But things have changed," Kim added

Kim's cell phone range. She glanced at the displayed number. "Work. It's Rex."

"Rex? What's up?" Kim asked into the cellphone.

"Where are you?" The Agent known as T-Rex asked. "We need you back at the office. Something new just came up."

"Just leaving the Zoo," Kim said. "Hank is going to do some forensic testing for us on the fur and hair sample."

"Good, say 'Hi' to the Big Man for me. Now beat feet back. See you in a few," he directed.

"Copy that." Kim disconnected the call, looked at Hank. "Gotta go. Duty calls. Rex says, 'Hi.'"

"Tell him, 'Hi' back. He's a good man."

Kim let out a small sigh. "He's like a 'Dutch Uncle' to me a lot of the time," Kim explained. "Makes me recognize uncomfortable truths."

Kim reached out, clasped Hanks hand. "Can we continue this conversation later?"

"Sure, Tiger Lady," Hank replied.

Hearing how he said 'Tiger Lady' made her feel some familiar butterflies in her stomach. She mentally slapped them down. What was happening to her?"

Kim smiled at Hank, then said, "You be careful around those large predators, Hank."

"And you, Kim, be careful around the

two-legged kind."

"Yes. That is the problem, isn't it?"

She drove back to the SAC Office in silence. She was glad she was by herself, had time to think. The passion she felt for John Wang-God, it was intense. But now she suddenly was questioning it. That reaction of Madam Chou— Kim knew John had his fingers in many a pie, knew what was going on in much of 'Chinatown.' But was she ignoring that some of those pies might involve bad apples? That John walked some sort of tightrope between law enforcement and the criminal element? Rex said he was a great politician. And many a politician dabbled in and dealt with the 'dark side.' This was one of the significant problems her father had to handle in his business relationships with many a country. Government Officials had a strong tendency toward corruption. Power corrupts, just like Lord Acton said many years ago.

As Kim pulled into the parking garage, she knew she had some serious decisions to make. And one of those decisions was... who could she confide in??

25.

K im, Rex, and all the Agents on the Title III met with the supervisors in the SAC Conference Room. Deputy SAC Brad Ball was in the head position at the long table, ran the meeting.

"All right. Tom Gill is on the secure telephone to Headquarters, trying to both PUT out some fires as well as get some updated intelligence info from the 'dark side.' Seems the raids set off a large crap storm-Kelly, you want to tell everyone here what your technical equipment caught? By the way, this is classified Confidential, does NOT leave this room."

Kelly Olivet stood up, cut straight to the chase. Attached to the grease writing board was a map of Downtown Seattle.

"Matt Swenson obtained a court order to use a StingRay cellular capture unit. Thus, every time someone talked on a cell phone anywhere in the coverage area, the call and its information was routed through the StingRay unit as it replaced the normal cell phone tower for the transmitter and router of the call." He paused for a minute to let the information sink in.

"A whole lot of information buzzed around this area." He pointed to an area that included The Jade Palace. Kim's stomach flipped flopped a bit.

"Well, we've obtained a few new cell numbers to include in the trap and trace. But, the people we are targeting are not new to the game. They are using disposable phones. And one in particular, who we think is the person identified as 'The Boss,' is using a high tech crypto phone or phones. These tell him when his call is being captured by StingRay. Plus, he has a form of encryption on his, or hers, voice communications. Texting from that specific phone is encoded, but people who text to that phone is not. So, we know what Madam Chou was sending him. However, someone was in a hurry and sent a reply that was not encrypted, might have been a short glitch in the system. Thus, we know The Boss sent the order to dispose of the bodies. Murphy's Law was on our side for once."

There was a bit of murmuring from the assembled personnel.

"Matt, you want to tell him what you found?" Kelly asked.

Matt Swenson stood up. "Headquarters has verified that someone is mounting a Cyber Attack against our computer system."

"You mean the Office, or the DHS/ICE network?" Rex asked.

"Both. As these hit us, the attacks tried to find a link into the main network."

The silence could be cut with a knife, just like the legendary saying. For the Agents in the room knew that such a concerted attack usually meant an intelligence arm of a foreign government. Now, they were not just facing some criminal enterprise, they may be involved with a significant foreign government agency, with all the attached threats and ramifications. Some foreign governments were known to be just as violent as *Narco Trafficantes* and the Russian Mafia, but with even more significant resources.

Matt continued. "So, we are coordinating everything through D.C., as well as having to work with all the federal intelligence agencies, to include NSA, DIA, CIA and the FBI."

"Regular alphabet soup," mumbled Rex.

"The one nice thing is any existing traditional 'Chinese Wall' that exists between law enforcement, and the intelligence community disappears in a situation like this,' advised Matt. "A Cyber-attack such as this can be classified as a National Security Threat."

Matt continued. "Because of that, we already have another targeted location identified for a search warrant, Rex has sent his Surveillance Team with the van to that address, will sit on it through the night. We'll hit it at Oh Dark Thirty in the morning. The federal warrant is being signed as we speak."

"May I ask where it's located?" Kim said.

Mat pointed to a spot on the map that was a mere two blocks from the Jade Palace.

"Empty office building, supposedly empty anyways. Owners are listed as the Red Star Import Export Corporation, just like the limo."

Kim sat silent. There was way too much activity around the areas where John Wang was active and owned properties. Plus, how could the President of the

Seattle Asian Business Association NOT have some kind of idea, at least a hint of organized criminal activity? Kim would have to do some of her own snooping, under the radar. She didn't want to make serious accusations against her paramour without definite proof.

Matt continued. "We should have a search warrant this evening. Then, the Operations Plan for the entry and search."

He paused. "Look it, thanks to us hitting the two locations today, the 'enemy' will be on high alert. The criminals involved in this may just try and disappear. Or, there may be something in this last location they are willing to either fight for or destroy due to possible evidence against their operations. So as they say, we have to stay frosty. Rex."

"Yes, Matt."

"Can you help me put together the Search Warrant Team, get all the other back-up from other agencies?" The Senior Agent asked.

"Of course."

ASAC Weiss jumped in. "Look it. This turning into one helluva investigation. This office will really be put on all the maps in the world, make the evening news over this. So remember. Silence is golden. Communications and operations security is a must. Any tip-offs, even to the Press, could get someone killed or at least completely screw up any prosecution. Everyone clear on that? Good. Get your stuff organized. We'll have the Search Warrant Briefing as soon as possible."

All the Special Agents headed to their respective desks and offices. As Kim walked to hers, Supervisor Salmon stopped her.

"Kupar. In my office. Now."

Kim followed him into his office. "Shut the door," he ordered.

Kim did as she was told, then stayed standing.

"Sit down."

"Excuse me, Sir, but what is this about?" she asked.

Salmon glared at her. "I know you've been running around in the Asian community, seemed to be a magnet for trouble."

"Sir?"

"Well, I'm not going to be held responsible for a female Agent getting herself into trouble, hurt," Salmon barked. "You're going to wait the rest of this investigation out. I've got some paperwork you can get caught up on—"

Kim began to anger. "And just who do you have who speaks Mandarin?" she questioned. "You know this is connected to Mainland China."

"I'll find someone. That's it!" The Supervisor commanded. You will not argue with me. I'm in charge..."

"I think the SAC and Deputy Sac are calling the shots right now," Kim declared. "And I know they need a Mandarin speaker NOW. Not next week!"

Salmon exploded. "Who in the fuck do you think you are? Another little girl who barges into a man's job tried to throw her weight around! That's all you are. A troublemaker, who gets into brawls in the street..."

"I was attacked, you arrogant fool! " Kim stepped toward Salmon's desk as she raged back. "I saved a woman's life. While you sat on your ass!"

Salmon's face went white with anger. "I'll have your badge, your ass..."

"You'll have nothing." Kim leaned in toward him and hissed. "Fire me. Go ahead. If you can. I can make my own way in the world!"

Now her face was inches from his. "But I think EEO and OPR will want to hear about a man who calls a minority woman a "girl", then threatens her."

Salmon sputtered, blanched. "Don't, don't, don't you threaten ME!"

"That is not a threat, that is a promise!" Kim spat out.

Just then, someone pounded on the door.

"Hey, can you hold it down in there?" It was Rex. "You're spoiling my coffee!"

"Go away!" Salmon yelled, having someone else to deflect his anger and frustration at.

"This is not over, Agent!" He glared at Kim, trying to act as if he were in control.

Kim laughed. At the derisive laugh, Salmon's face turned a beet red. He jerked to standing, ranted.

"I ought to kick your ass!"

Kim laughed again, spat out a reply. "Fine. I'll be waiting." She turned around in one swift move, then marched out of the office. She did not slam the door, leaving it open as Salmon sputtered and swore at his desk.

Rex was standing in the hall nearby. "Hey, Kim—" he started to speak.

"Leave me alone!" Kim snapped at him, kept marching, eyes straight ahead. In moments, she was in the Ladies Room.

Kim looked in the mirror, saw the tears of rage come. She then did what could be seen as a stereotypical move of the male gender. She stepped over and kicked a stall door so hard that one of the hinges broke loose.

"Fuck!" she swore. Why her? Why was this all happening now? John, Hank, Salmon-males in her life, causing her grief.

"Why can't they just leave me alone?" Kim said to herself.

A hand with polished nails handed her a Kleenex. Kim looked at Anne Knudsen. The female supervisor smiled, then asked, "Couldn't help but overhear some of that. Want a witness?"

Kim took the Kleenex, patted at the tears. "No. Not now. It would just escalate things." The unspoken thought was one escalation might be to draw attention to her relationship with John Wang. Until she had some time to think, check out some of the uncertainties she now had about who did what in 'Chinatown,' she did not want OPR or someone else asking questions involving her and John.

Anne nodded and spoke. "You are not the first woman who had to deal with Dave Salmon. He has a 'short man's complex' so bad that in Wikipedia, there is a photo of him next to the definition."

This made Kim chuckle. "And he thinks he can take it out on women," she stated.

Anne shrugged. "Why not? A man he attacked like that might risk their job and smack him," the female Supervisor explained. "We women rarely result to that. At least in my generation."

"But us younger women—" commented Kim.

"In your case, Kim, I know you can give as good as you get. I'm surprised Salmon did not notice that."

Kim sniffed. "I don't want to get a reputation as an out of control bully, just because I can physically take care of myself," she explained.

Now Anne chuckled. "No matter what you do, you, as a female, are going to be open to additional scrutiny and criticism, plus gossip."

"Ma'am. How did he get and keep his job?" Kim asked. "I mean. With such a negative attitude, especially toward women—"

"Call me Anne. And he is a prime example of the Peter Principle and bureaucratic inertia. He sucked up to the right person, was promoted, and then found he was in over his head. But no one wants to take the time to deal with him. So, he gets transferred to D.C., where he can be shuffled around to jobs where he'll do the least damage."

The Group Supervisor paused in thought, then continued. "I guess some may say that about me sometimes. But at least I don't go off on people, yell at them because I'm insecure." She smiled at Kim.

"Anyways, you hang in there," stated Anne. "You're showing that you are a fine Agent. We need to keep you here."

Kim smiled, a bit self-conscious. "Can I ask you one more question?" she queried.

"Sure. Go ahead."

"In this job... how do you balance your social life? I mean, you have to worry who you associate with, make sure they're not trying to use your position for their own improvement."

"Kim, I was lucky," Anne replied. "I knew my husband before I became a Special Agent. I knew I could trust him."

Anne then laughed. "But ole T-Rex told me one day that when he was young, in the Military, he was warned about 'booze, broads, and bills.' Well, change the 'broads' to 'boys,' and it can apply to us. Infatuation causing a person to think with their genitals rather than their brains is an equal opportunity problem. It applies to everyone, no exceptions for gender and sexual orientation."

Kim stood silent, thinking. What Anne had said was so right. Was she sacrificing something of herself for infatuation with John, or was it a regular love affair? And did John have a hidden agenda? God, *now* she starts to examine the situation!

"Thanks for the talk, Anne," she told the Supervisor. "It's nice to know that you're not the only woman to deal with these things."

Anne squeezed her hand, said, "You hang in there, Young Lady. We need more young people like you. You're the next generation of ICE Investigations."

Anne left Kim standing in front of the mirror. So much had happened, so much to think about. Well, she couldn't stay hidden in there. Kim washed her face, reapplied a very light make-up and checked her hair. Then, back to work.

She stepped out of the Ladies Room, saw Rex standing further down the hall. He turned his head toward her.

"Everything okay?" he asked

"Nothing I can't handle, T-Rex."

He smiled. "That's my Raptor," he praised. "Come on, Matt and I are putting together the tactics for the raid. Come on and get some training experience."

"Okay, Sound's fun."

As they walked down the hallway, Kim realized that she had friends here, like Matt and T-Rex, who had her back. She felt good. Salmon could go screw himself.

26.

It was Oh Dark Thirty, and the Entry Team quickly formed up around the corner from the target empty office building. Or at least the location was supposedly unoccupied, no registered businesses operating from any of the vacant offices. Kim was Number Three in the 'stack' with Dennis Spain as the Tactical Shield Man the first, Matt Swenson was in the second position as Team Leader, with Rex Moyer directly behind Kim. Six more Agents were behind Kim, everyone arrayed in tactical vests, body armor, and weapons. Rex had an MP-5, was a certified instructor in it, with a couple other Agents with shotguns and one with an M-4 Assault Rifle.

Matt, an Entry Tactics Instructor, had tried to put Kim on the Perimeter Security Team. She had stared at him.

"So let me get this straight. You have another Mandarin Speaker handy?" Questioned Kim.

"Well, no. But..."

"And of course you have someone with Big Cat experience, right? I mean, we keep coming up with fur and hair samples, so a Bengal or its first cousin *must* be in one of these locations..."

"Oh, all right!" Matt acquiesced. "You win. I'll put you on the Entry Team. Sheesh, I was just trying to be a..."

"A male chauvinist. So you and Rex can just stop treating me like your little sister. Got it?"

She knew she was coming off as pissed at them, but dammit, she was pissed. After Salmon's attempt to demean her, all the other confusion and conflict she was not about to take crap from anyone.

Rex looked at Matt. "See what I have to put up with? Thank your stars you're not her Training Agent anymore."

T-Rex then looked at Kim. "It's you funeral, Agent. Just remember that."

In Mandarin, she replied, *"Yes, Uncle, I know."*

"What?"

"I said, 'Yes, Sir.'"

"Yeah, sure you did."

Matt gave the order "Move," and they did. In one coordinated action, they were at a secondary door just down from the glassed-in main entrance, which would have made them big fat targets at the double doors had they entered there. There was no glass on the secondary entrance, and the deadbolt was cheap. As they neared, Don Johnson worked his way up with the large metal ram and positioned himself off to the side of the door. Back around the corner of the building was the secondary team made up of SPD SWAT and VICE Squad members. After the ICE Agents had entered and secured the main floor and stairwell, the second team would enter and secure the office space on the upper levels.

Matt nodded to Don, who used his fist to pound three times on the door. Matt called out *"Police! Federal agents with a search warrant! open up!"*

Matt and Don Johnson repeated these actions three times in a space of some ten seconds. No response. Matt looked at Don and said: "Ram It."

The big Agent used his strength and bulk to swing the ram, striking the door just above the cheap deadbolt. The door flew open and Dennis Spain was through with the Tactical Shield before the door could swing back. Matt was glued to his ass, and all the rest of the Agents followed suit. Within seconds the Entry Team was in the hallway, walking fast to the foyer of the glass-doored main entrance with a minimum of noise

Kim thought she heard an unfamiliar 'pinging' noise just as Matt began to yell "Police" once again. Then strong arms were grabbing her and propelling her to the floor as T-Rex bellowed in her ear *"Bomb! Boobytrap!"* Her hearing was overloaded with a loud explosion. Kim lay stunned on the office building tiled floor, ears ringing, with a heavy weight on her. It took her a moment to realize it was Rex. She thought she heard a muffled voice screaming *"Agents down! Agents down!"* through the ringing but she was having trouble focusing, her vision blurry.

She felt herself lifted up, cradled as if she were a child and carried out to the city sidewalk. Rex set her down, her back against the building. Her blurred vision began to clear, and Rex's face was in front of hers.

"Can you hear me, Kim?"

"Yeah. My ears are ringing. "

"Hold still while I check you for injuries," Rex instructed.

With clinical precision, Rex gently but also firmly patted her entire body, as well as looked for blood.

"No blood, no bones sticking out. Here. Souvenir."

He placed a piece of jagged metal in her hand.

"Your helmet stopped it," he explained. "Now you know why I insisted everyone was fitted for one."

Kim stared at the metal evidence of violence.

"The rest of the team—" she began to say.

"You worry about yourself. We had EMTs standing by. They're here now."

"No, I need to..." She tried to stand up. Rex stopped her.

"You need to follow your Training Agent's orders, dammit. Now, SIT!" The Senior Agent ordered

She looked into his eyes, saw the pressing concern. Then she remembered.

"You pushed me out of the way, threw yourself top of me. Why?"

"That's what Partners do. I'd do it for anybody, so don't get all swell headed—"

She began to blink back tears. "Thanks," she choked out.

"Oh Hell!" exclaimed Rex. "Turn off the waterworks. Now stay sitting. Or else. I need to check on the others."

As Kim sat, as the ringing subsided, an EMT came over and checked her out. The young blonde was calm and efficient in her duties. She smiled when her check was complete.

"You're good,' said the EMT. "You may have a

headache for a while. Ringing stopped in your ears?"

"Yes, Ma'am," Kim Answered. "Thanks."

"Name is Susan. Susan Rand. You're Kim Kupar, right?"

"Why, yes. How did you know my name?" Kim asked.

"Responded that day when the Chinese Guy had his brains blown out," Susan Rand answered. "Then you made the news. Heard you helped that Vietnamese girl."

"Just doing my job. Like you."

"Well, keep doing it, please," the EMT added. "Nice to show all the men in the world what we can do when given the chance."

Kim frowned. "Men. My team—"

Susan's expression became serious. "Yeah, gotta go—"

Kim grabbed her arm. "Dammit, what's wrong?" she demanded

Susan looked into her eyes. Kim noticed that Susan's eyes were tearing up.

"We... lost one. I'm sorry," the EMT softly said, looking down.

"Who? Dammit WHO!!!"

Just then, Tim Weiss walked up. "I got this, young lady."

"Yes, Sir. Stay Safe, Kim." Susan rose and walked off. Kim started to stand, and the ASAC knelt beside her.

"Just stay sitting, Kim. Please."

"Who was it?" Kim asked. "Who did we lose?"

Weiss paused. "We-it was Matt..."

"NO!!" Kim cried out. "Let me up! I—"

"There was nothing anyone could do, Kim. A piece of metal entered the base of his skull, under his helmet," explained the ASAC. "He didn't know what hit him."

Kim began to cry. Then to sob. Rex walked up.

"I got it, Boss," he told Weiss.

"Let me know if you need anything. You two hang in there," said Weiss as he walked away with slumped shoulders. Rex knelt down next to Kim.

"It should have been me, Rex. I don't have any kids. No wife—" She sobbed more.

"Hey, Raptor. It should not have been anybody. But it was. People, friends die in this job," stated the older man.

Rex swallowed hard, then reached out and hugged Kim. "It hurts, Kim. It always does."

27.

K im sat in her townhouse, stared at the wall. Everyone involved in the Raid was given time off, no matter if injured or not. They were allowed to write their after action reports as they felt up to it. Seattle's Finest had finished the search, with no more booby traps. At Kim's request, the Evidence Collection Teams had looked for any types of fur or hair, as well as any documents in Mandarin.

They had found both. Not to mention the explosives used had been 'Chicom' grenades of a current military issue, bundled together with a trip wire and connected to a central pin. EOD personnel said it was a near miracle that only Matt Swenson had been killed by all the shrapnel flying around.

Kim had snuck into the office after hours and convinced Allen White to let her look at the collected evidence. She saw the Bengal Cat had been there in the building. And she had seen some familiar writing on one of the documents. Every person who writes in any language will have some unique characteristics of their penmanship. And now she sat in her home, with a copy of a page in Mandarin concerning a large animal to be imported.

The writing looked like John Wang's.

Kim sat on her couch, kept comparing the script to some love notes on a couple of greeting cards he had given her, as well as the business card where he had written his personal line on. The matches were just too close. She may not be a handwriting expert, but in the business world, you paid attention to handwriting. Her Father had taught her that. Her mind went back to the previous days-

Matt Swenson's Funeral was the day before. Police and Law Enforcement from all over the Nation, as well as from Canada and some other foreign police agencies, sent representatives. The President of the United States stated he planned to come until he talked to Pat Swenson. She asked him not to, afraid it would turn into a media circus due to the misgivings about China. So, the President contacted some of his business friends, and they set up a Go Fund Me page on the Internet to help both Matt's Widow and the children, as well as a separate fund for the victims of Human Trafficking.

At the funeral, after the processions, official words of condolences, and 'Amazing Grace' on the bagpipes, Kim had approached Pat and the children. She had the newest born, Patricia, their first daughter, in her arms, The two little boys, Matt Junior, age six, and Michael, age five, were standing by their mother. Nearby were both sets of Grand Parents.

Kim walked up, and Pat smiled as she greeted her.

"Hey, stranger. Glad to see you." Matt had always referred to his wife as a "trooper" who never let anything get her down.

Kim tried not to lose her composure. "Pat-I'm so sorry. I—" More words just would not come. Tears began to well up in her eyes, which Pat quickly noticed. The deceased Agents wife motioned toward her parents and asked them if they could watch the grandchild for a few minutes, to which they readily agreed. She then took Kim by the hand and led her to some chairs away from the hubbub of the funeral.

As they sat, Kim began to cry. "I should have said something, done something. I had a feeling something was wrong."

Pat held her hands in both of hers. "Matt and I knew the dangers. He gave me three beautiful children, so much love—"

Pat blinked back tears. "Matt considered you as a good friend. As I still do. So, don't go beating yourself up, blaming yourself for the actions of some sick bastards. They did this, not you."

Kim knew, though that someone else close to her may be involved. She felt so very guilty for not seeing some of the signs of John's possible involvement, or at least him hiding suspicions or knowledge of the criminal element in 'his' Asian community.   All due to some misguided code of silence.

Kim looked into Pat's eyes.

"Is there anything I can do?" she asked. "Anyway, I can help?"

Pat straightened in her chair a bit. "Yes, there is," the widow answered. "Matt said you were one of the most motivated and hardworking Agents in the office.

He said once you got your teeth into something, you did not let go. He used the expression of worrying an investigation like an old bone. I think he got that expression from T-Rex."

Pat squeezed Kim's hands as she continued. "Get these bastards. Get these scum who took the love of my life from me. Made my children fatherless. Please. You can do that for me, Kim. Yes, just that."

Kim brought her thoughts back to the present. She looked at the copies of the evidence and reports once more. Hank had verified that all the fur and hair samples came from just one 'Big Cat.' It was a large feline of a unique species, with genetically tweaked and combined DNA that seemed to scream out "Frankenstein" every time she looked at it. She could not see the purpose behind it. How could smuggling of exotic animals have any connection with Human Trafficking?

Someone buzzed her intercom to be let it. Kim almost did not answer it but knew it might be someone from the office checking up on her. She had let cellphone calls go to voicemail many times, not wanting to talk to anyone. That had included several attempts by John Wang to call her. Texts went unanswered. But something nagged at her that she needed to see who this was, who asked for entry into her home of darkness.

"Yes?"

"Kim, it's me. A.J. I—I need to talk."

"If this is an attempt to cheer me up—" Kim began to answer.

"No! Please. Let me up!" A.J. pleaded.

Kim frowned. He sounded so agitated, especially for ole happy-go-lucky A.J. She buzzed him up.

She opened the door before he even had the chance to knock.

"This had better be good—" and froze. Standing a bit behind, A.J. was Jade.

"What in Holy Hell do you think you are doing?" she declared. "Why is Jade-?"

A.J. barged into her townhouse, yanking Jade in with him.

"Quick. Shut the door!" he ordered. "I don't think anyone followed us—"

Kim shut the door and threw the deadbolt on. For A.J. to be this agitated, this scared, there must be a grave reason. A.J. Took Jade directly to the couch, where she began to cling to him, her eyes wide in fear.

"All right. Spit it out, at least one of you," demanded Kim. "I have too much serious crap going on in my life to be involved with some other bovine excrement-

"*I am to be given to Sir Kahn!*" Jade blurted out in Mandarin, then began to cry. A.J. hugged her.

"*Sir Kahn is a large tiger, isn't he?*" Asked Kim in Mandarin.

Jades teary eyes went wide.

"*Master Wang has told you?? Oh no! I'm not safe here!*" Jade tried to get up, but A.J. held on.

"*Hey, Jade. This is my Big Sister. You can trust her,*" assured A.J.

Kim walked over to the couple, sat down in the padded chair facing the couch.

"*I know because an investigation we are involved in has turned up 'Big Cat' fur,*" she explained. "*It involves Human Trafficking also. Which you have personal experience with, right, Jade?*"

Jade could only nod her head vigorously.

"*Sis, I knew you could help!*" Declared A.J. "*There just is nowhere else for us to hide. John Wang has feelers connections everywhere!*"

Kim's cell phone rang. She looked at the number. It was John, calling from his personal line.

Shit. She knew she had to take this. She looked at the frightened couple. "*It's John Wang. Be quiet.*"

Kim walked into the kitchen. "*Hello, John.*"

"*My Jade Beauty!*" The voice on the phone said. "*I have been so worried. I know you do not feel like talking, but...*"

Kim was a mass of conflicting feelings. One second love, the next anger, all aimed at the man she thought she knew.

"*Yes, you're right. But I also understand your caring about me.*"

"*I didn't go to the funeral of Agent Swenson as I know that the Chinese government may have a connection to his death,*" her lover explained. "*So, the Asian Community, at my suggestion, sent a large wreath expressing our condolences. I knew Matt Swenson through Rex. He was a credit to his community and your agency.*"

"*Yes, he was, John,*" agreed Kim. "*And now some bastards killed him, left a widow and three small children behind.*"

"*If there is anything I can do to help—*" began John.

"*How about getting the Asian Community to turn over those responsible? Or at least tell me what they know about them?*"

John Wang paused. Kim could almost see the wheels turning, trying to figure out what to say to allay her anger.

"I will put feelers out, dearest, "he finally replied. "I can at least do that. Plus, I can pressure my employees to tell me what they know if they wish to stay in my employ."

"Thank You, John. I'm-sorry I am so short, so curt with you," Kim said. "But I lost a good friend. And it happened in your Asian Community."

"I understand," replied John. "Please, I will help as best I can. Believe me, your pain causes me pain. So, ask, and I'll do whatever I can to help you."

Kim paused for a moment before she replied. She decided she was going to take a chance.

"I did hear about someone called Sir Kahn. Not a common Chinese name."

Silence at the other end. Kim now knew she had mentioned something that was a secret. And even John Wang was taken aback. This secret must be HUGE.

"I, I will check. Where did you hear this unusual name?" For once, John had uncertainty in his voice

"John, you know I can't reveal official sources. I'm taking a chance mentioning it to you, out of school like Americans say."

"English speaking Americans, Kim. For we are both citizens, are we not?"

Kim thought that she did not really know what kind of citizen John was if he was as involved in this mess as much as she was led to believe by her suspicions.

"I must go now, John. I need to check in with my office," Kim excused.

"Of Course. When will I be able to see you again?" His voice had a bit of a pleading tone.

"I'm not very friendly right now, John. Please give me a couple of days," requested Kim. "Okay?"

"Of course, my jade-eyed beauty. Just remember I am always here for you." John's voice still sounded like he was uncertain, unsure.

"Yes. I will. Bye now." Kim disconnected the call, stood staring at the telephone. She began to feel a bit cold inside.

"Big Sister, you okay?" A.J. asked.

"No, I am not," Kim replied in English. "I am beginning to think nothing is as it seems."

"Well, I'm here for you,' A.J. stated in English. "That does not change."

Kim looked at him. "And you bring questions in the form of Jade here."

She walked over and sat in front of Jade, looked intently into her face.

"Young Lady," declared Kim. "You need to tell me everything that happened, that you know. And no, you will not be arrested for being in the U.S. illegally. You are as much a victim as all the others smuggled in for labor, drugs and sex."

Approximately a quarter hour later, Kim had a sound vision of what had been occurring under the noses of the authorities for at least a year. Jade (not her real name of course) had been smuggled into the United States some three months prior. She relayed that two young women had died due to what sounded like botulism poisoning in the container in which they were smuggled into the Port of Seattle. The Boss had taken a liking to her from the start, began to groom her for bigger and better things.

The Boss was John Wang.

When Kim heard her suspicions verified, a cold icicle seemed to penetrate her stomach and spine. The man she thought she loved was one of the worst criminals in existence. John dealt with the equivalent of 19th Century slavery, bringing in primarily young women and girls into the U.S. for use as sex slaves, indentured servitude and as 'mules' for the smuggling of whatever contraband John and his associates needed to move. He also brought in the occasional young boy, to be sold to a small circle of pedophiles who paid premium prices for the young flesh.

"How do you know all this, Jade? Why would he confide all these details with you?"

"He liked me, said I was smarter than the rest, better education," the young Chinese lady answered. "And… my eyes."

"You mean your jade eyes? That is where you got your new name from, right?" Kim asked.

"He has a fixation with jade eyes," Jade answered. "He uses his contacts within the Asian community to hunt for any and all women with jade eyes. I heard of the Vietnamese girl you saved. She was to be delivered to Master Wang as payment for some outstanding debt."

"You mean he was working with the Vietnamese gangs, not in competition with them?" Kim bored in.

"He works with all Asians. Japanese, Vietnamese, Koreans… anyone with a criminal organization."

Kim paused for a moment, watching Jade. She was so well spoken. Kim knew she was not just some poor peasant girl sold off by her family, or taken from them, for some monetary debt. There was something else going on here.

"Jade, you are well educated, were in the equivalent of our secondary school when you were taken. Yes?" queried the Special Agent.

Jade looked down, mumbled. "I was not taken. I was given."

Kim stopped in shock. "You mean to pay off a debt," she declared.

"No," replied Jade. "My father-he wanted a higher position in the Chinese Mainland Government. He also wanted a son. So, he gave me to the Chinese officials connected to Master Wang. For that, he received more power. And a son whose parents had been executed for some misdeed against the government was officially declared my father's. No adoption. It was as if the previous parents ceased to exist, were never there."

Kim had heard many a strange story due to her families business, and then her position as a Special Agent, but this! A father to give his own daughter away as if she never existed, just to climb the social and power ladder. It was just sick. As frustrated as her father may have become with Kim for her lack of joining him in the family business as he wished. Even that she became a 'Cop' instead, no way would he have ever thought of using her to curry those in power. Or to also disown her as some older, traditional cultures may.

A.J. jumped into the conversation. "That's just the tip of the old iceberg, Kim. Jade, tell him about the animals and such."

Kim looked at Jade, continued to question. "Yes. This Sir Kahn is some type of Bengal—"

"No! He is not natural! He is a monster!" Jade cried out, then began to shake and cry. A.J. put his arms around her and she collapsed into him, sobbing. Right then, Kim saw the love and affection between the two younger people. She suddenly began to feel old, as well as very sad. One moment, she had a person she thought was her love of her life, as well as a good friend as a mentor. The next, they were both gone, one dead physically, the other dead to her emotionally. Yet A.J. and Jade, amid all this turmoil and what Kim could see was a growing evil, had found each other and love.

"So, can one of you tell me what you know about this?" Kim continued. "Time is of the essence. I can't allow any more people to be hurt or killed."

Jade made an effort and managed to compose herself. "As you noticed, I was well educated."

She dabbed her eyes with a tissue A.J. had found, then looked at Kim as she spoke. "I was in what here would be accelerated studies for gifted students. I was being groomed for a career in the biological sciences. That included basic training in genetics."

Jade swallowed. Kim interrupted. "A.J., can you make us some tea?"

"Sure, Kim." As A.J. went to obtain the tea, Jade began again.

"When I was given away, no thought about my training or background was considered. I suddenly found myself in among young women and girls from all walks of life, shoved into a shipping container kicking and screaming. I soon found such resistance was futile."

"Then you had a not so nice sea voyage here, as you said before."

"Yes, Kim. Then I met... the Boss, John Wang. He is an excellent judge of character, could tell I was not some ignorant farm girl. During our early conversations, he found out about my science background, became very pleased that, as he put it, 'finally I have someone intelligent enough to understand my plans and projects.'

That is when he showed me-Sir Kahn." As she again mentioned the Tiger's name, Jade began to shake a bit. She made a visible effort and regained her composure as she continued.

"Sir Kahn started as a Bengal Tiger. Now, he is something else."

"Jade, I worked up close with the Big Cats. Tell me how he is different."

"He is larger," Jade answered. "His fur is more brown and black, little striping. And his fangs—" Jade shook again.

A.J. came back with some hot tea. "Sorry. Instant rather than steeped."

"That's okay," said Kim. "Jade, I know this is hard, but I need all the details. Please."

Jade took a sip of the proffered tea. Straightened her back as she replied.

"I know. I must do this. Sir Kahn's fangs, teeth. They have been extremely elongated through genetic manipulation. He looks like pictures from a book I saw in our school library. Sir Kahn looks like a Sabre Tooth Tiger."

Kim swore. She swore in three different languages. She swore at the situation and her blindness to the unique form of madness that must be part of John, her object of passion and love.

"Hey, Big Sister!" Exclaimed A.J. "I haven't seen you this angry in years!"

Kim took charge of her emotions, looked at A.J. as she spoke.

"That is because this is a special type of evil. John Wang is trying to create mutations for the exotic animal smuggling market. And he is using endangered species to do it. That is bad enough. But when you start dealing with creating extinct predators, you are asking for trouble."

A.J. frowned. "Regular Tigers are dangerous," he proffered.

"Think 'Jurassic Park' in real life, Brother. When Sabre Tooth Cats existed, we were looked on as just another big monkey to eat," Kim explained. "Predators had no developed fear of humankind."

Kim paused, took a sip of her tea. "I have no idea what prey drive John Wang may have instilled in this large feline through his genetic tampering. But you and the others are deathly afraid of him, Jade. Because John used Sir Kahn as a special enforcer. Yes?"

Jade tried to hold back the tears as her voice shook. "People who displeased Master Wang were given to Sir Kahn—for his pleasure."

Jade swallowed, hard. "The sound of those huge fangs penetrating bone, skull... I will never forget!"

Kim stared at Jade. "He made you WATCH?" Blurted Kim.

"He said I had the intelligence and training to understand what he was doing," a quavering Jade answered. "So, he had me watch."

Kim sat and stared off into space for a moment. She began to feel as if she had been dumped into some grade 'B' movie with the monsters created from mad computer graphics. But this was real.

"God Help us, A.J. This is madness," she said.

"That is not all, Big Sister. Jade, honey, tell her the rest," coaxed A.J.

Jade looked down once again. She took another sip from her tea, looked at it as she spoke.

"Do you have anything... harder?"

"Like Scotch?"

"Yes, that will do."

Kim jumped up, went to her cupboard and grabbed the bottle of top end Scotch she had bought and shared with John Wang at what seemed now ages ago. She threw ice cubes in glasses, poured in the Scotch, went back to the living room.

"Here," Kim offered. "This should go down smooth."

Jade took a large drink of the Scotch and surprised Kim by not choking. "He is also working on modifications on humans," declared Jade.

"What the—" stammered Kim.

"He is fixated on jade green eyes, Kim. Said they are so gorgeous, most women should have them. So, he collects girls and women with jade eyes, studies their genetic makeup. He wanted to make them the dominant genetic eye color."

Kim stared at the young Asian woman again. "So I was part of a -collection?" A chill went through Kim as she asked.

Jade looked into Kim's eyes, then spoke. "You are special to him. I think he hoped to one day to convince you to be part of his 'project.' And his empire. For he IS building an empire in Seattle."

"Like Hell, he will!" Kim blurted out. She downed her Scotch, stood up, and began pacing. She was so goddamned angry. At the situation, at herself. T-Rex had warned her about people taking advantage of her due to her position. Yet, despite the warning, she had fallen headlong into the trap. Why did she not put two and two together, that John Wang always seemed to know what law enforcement was doing, yet claimed ignorance of the crimes around him?

"I'm a damned lovesick puppy!" She cried out, angry tears welling up into her eyes. Then A.J. was hugging her.

"Hey, Sis. It'll be alright. I love you, the family loves you. I know you'll figure this out," A.J. consoled his Big Sister.

She turned and hugged him back. Funny how her ne'er do well Little Brother had so much confidence in her abilities. But it gave her some feelings of security, knowing she at least had this kind of love in her life.

She let go of A.J., walked over, and sat down next to Jade. She took Jade's hands in her own as she spoke.

"I know this is very hard and scary to you, Jade. I'm glad you came forward. I promise I'll make sure you're protected."

Jade shrugged. "I know that my fate may be sealed. Master Wang—"

"Don't give him the respect of the title of 'Master'!" Ordered Kim. "He is a sick, scum bag."

Verbalizing that feeling seemed to help, made the acceptance of lost love a bit easier. However, only a bit.

"You and A.J. will stay here," Kim told the couple. "I need to go to the office, type up a quick report while all this is fresh in my mind. Then, I call out the Calvary."

Kim strode over to the coat closet near the front door, reached up and pulled a wooden box from its hiding place. She set the box on the coffee table in front of Jade and A. J., opened the box, and displayed its contents.

"Remember this, Little Brother?"

"Hell yeah!" Exclaimed A.J. "The Howdah pistol

you shot that Bengal with, saved Uncle Abe. I wondered if you still had it."

"It's cap and ball, a black powder antique, so it's legal in this state. I'm going to load it with fresh shot and powder, fresh percussion caps. You keep it here while I run the office," Kim instructed her brother. "This is the only personal weapon I have right now. I'm beginning to think I need T-Rex to help me buy some others."

Her brother picked up the pistol. "Yeah. I can handle this in a pinch."

"Okay. I load this beast, you stay here 'off' the cellphones," Kim warned. "No calls. John Wang may have the capability of tracing them. By the way, any idea where Sir Kahn is tonight?"

"There is a hidden cellar under the Jade Palace," offered the young Asian woman.

"I didn't know that," said A.J.

"Only-special people are allowed there. I am sure, with all the activity at Mas-I mean Wang's other properties where Sir Kahn has been kept, he will hide him there for the time being. He has keepers for the beast."

"Okay. Here we go," Kim said. "Jade, let me have your I.D. You are about to become a Confidential Informant in our system. I can get you paid for—"

"I want no blood money!" Jade cried out. "I do this-I don't want to hear crunching sounds, screams ever again. Though they may forever be in my nightmares."

28.

Kim used her code key to get into the office. She went to her desk, turned on, and then signed onto her government computer. Kim worked quickly, entered the essential stories from Jade into an ROI in the case file, and referred to a Confidential Informant. She'd have to get a registration identification number in the morning for Jade, to keep her identity entirely out of the system. She zipped through the necessary information on Jade, added it to a Confidential Informant Registration Form. Then, Kim placed it on T-Rex's desk for review. After that, it went into Salmon's office for approval, then up the chain. Kim was doing this as a complete Cover Her Ass (CYA) move so no one would accuse her of going off half-cocked. Also so that someone else had the information, in case something went wrong.

At that moment, something went wrong. Kim's cellphone rang, and she connected the call from A.J. All she heard were yells and a scream in Mandarin. Jade cried out, *"Not to Sir Kahn in the basement!"*

An angry voice in Mandarin told her to shut up. Next, the sound of a slap. The phone stayed connected long enough to for Kim to here Jade yell out once more about behind the maintenance room. Then silence.

She had heard what she thought was A.J.s voice yell, followed by what sounded like a violent struggle. Then nothing. She stared at the now silent telephone, her mind racing. If she called out the 'Cavalry' before she had any details about the location, all she would have would be a bunch of people rushing around, maybe tipping off Wang and putting the two young people in more danger. She would call T-Rex at least. He would have an idea. Before she could dial his number, an incoming call interrupted her. She did not recognize the number, answered, "Hello?"

It was John Wang.

"Kim?"

"Yes. I don't recognize this number—"

"New phone. We need to talk. Now."

"Why? It's late and—"

"I'm afraid something has happened to Jade. And it has to do with your investigation. Come down to the Jade Palace. I will meet you there." John hung up.

She stared at the telephone. Kim knew this was probably a setup. But she also knew that A.J. and Jade may soon be just so much butchered meat or flotsam and jetsam in Puget Sound. If she delayed too long, John would be suspicious, may 'off' the two young witnesses and disappear. If his organization was as large as Jade said it was, he probably had many contacts to help with an escape. Plus if she got ICE Investigation management involved at this minute, the inertia of government bureaucracy could delay action to a fatal amount.

"Shit." She ran out of the office, reset the alarm. As she scurried down the stairs to her G-Ride, she madly texted Rex with the basics of a dangerous situation, and to meet her at the Jade Palace. She did not want to take the time with a telephone conversation or have him order her to stand down. A text she could ignore for a while. Kim jumped into her Mustang, started to haul ass across town.

29.

THE JADE PALACE
INTERNATIONAL DISTRICT/CHINATOWN

Kim parked her Mustang in a small lot approximately a block and a half from the night club. It was just before Midnight, so only the bar area was still operating. She did not plan on entering the front of the club, especially after she saw a limousine and two large Asian Males in front of the entrance. She knew they were for her. Staying in the shadows, Kim snuck around to the alley behind the establishment. She had heard the comment about a maintenance room. Maybe it had an entrance or exit in the back? She hoped so.

Kim tried to adopt the gliding, silent stride of a real Bengal, staying on her toes as she snuck up the back of the Jade Palace. So far, so good. She found a door that looked like a delivery or employee entrance. The Gods were smiling as it was unlocked. There was no light on in the interior area behind the door, so she did not lose her night vision. Kim slowly crept into the building, her hand on her service weapon.

A large shape seemed to form in the darkness, then lunged at her. She was pulling her pistol from her holster when she saw stars. Then nothing.

Kim must have been 'out of it' for mere moments as she found herself held upright, strong hands clamped and immobilized her arms. The large being carried her in front, suspended some inches above the floor as if she were a life-sized doll.

"*I have her, Boss,*" a male voice rang out in Mandarin. The spoken words propelled Kim to action. She twisted and lashed out with her free legs and feet. The man holding her bellowed in pain, half dropped, half threw her down. Kim hit the floor and rolled, going for her still holstered sidearm. The distinct sound of an AK-47 bolt being racked back, let to slam forward came from behind her.

"*Pull that pistol, and you die,*" another male voice ordered in Mandarin.

Kim did an instantaneous review of the situation in her mind, took her hand slowly from her pistol.

"*Put your hands on your head,*" the same voice ordered. "*Samu, you big ox. Check her for weapons.*"

One of the largest Chinese men she had ever seen approached her from her front.

"*You kicked me.*" The Chinese called Samu was huge but had a boyish face. He reached out and yanked her primary weapon from its holster. He then proceeded to man-handle her. The man used large bear paw hands to squeeze, pull, pat, and tug the various parts of Kim's body. At the end of the rough search, Kim had her body armor pulled off, her baton, and both her pistols removed.

The man with the AK-47 prodded her in the back with the barrel.

"Walk straight ahead." Kim complied, scanning the area around her for possible escape routes. She knew she had gotten herself into deep *kimchee,* and now had to figure a way out.

She was prodded and shoved into a large room with cheap overhead fluorescent lights providing the illumination. There was sufficient light for her to see two Japanese men in expensive suits and ties toward one side of the room, and three younger Vietnamese males in silk jackets and colorful shirts near the other. As she was pushed into the center of the light, one of the Vietnamese stepped toward her.

"It's the whore," sneered the young man in English. "The whore who beat up my cousin in the alley. How does it feel to be on the receiving end—"

From the shadows stepped John Wang. He struck the Vietnamese young man with an open hand so hard that he knocked the man down. John stood above the fallen youth.

"You will keep a civil tongue in your head, Pigshit. Or you will have a date with Sir Khan."

He glared at the other two Vietnamese. "Control this fool. Or suffer the consequences."

"Yes, Boss," both men answered in unison.

John stepped toward Kim. He had a concerned look on his face.

"My Jade Beauty..."

"Don't! Don't you dare!" Kim spat out at John in Mandarin, *"How could you? After all, we said, did together? WHERE IS MY BROTHER?"* Kim ended screaming. Spittle from her rage hit John in his face. He stepped

back, sadness in his eyes. Samu grabbed her tight.

"*I am so very sorry, my love...*"

"*I am not your love! A true love does not hurt the one he loves. Not like this!*"

Kim knew all eyes were on her and John. She knew she was pushing the so-called envelope of the situation to its limits with her anger. But she could not help herself.

John Wang pulled a silk handkerchief from his suit pocket and wiped his face. He then folded it back and put it back into his upper suit pocket. John looked into her eyes as he spoke in English.

"Kim, I didn't want this. I was hoping to bring you in slowly, explain things to you. I am not an evil man."

Kim stared at him. "Are you serious?" she replied in kind with English.

"You smuggle humans as sex slaves. You smuggle exotic animals. You have people killed! You set bombs that killed my *friend!*" Kim began to scream again, then swallowed, controlled herself.

"Kim, I didn't mean anyone to be hurt, especially not killed," John tried to explain. "Only the few who have endangered my operations have I taken action against. You must realize that I also have people in China. I must answer to when it comes to the actions I have taken."

"Who? Slavers? People, who still keep *Kulis* as indentured servants? Or maybe people who enjoy making God's creatures into Frankenstein monsters." Kim's voice rose in intensity as she spoke.

John turned to the Japanese businessmen, spoke in English. "I am sorry, Mr. Yoshida. I did not see this situation spinning a bit out of control. Please believe me that after tonight, everything will be as it should be."

The fine dressed older man walked closer, gave a slight bow. "No need to apologize, my friend," Mr. Yoshida said in accent-less English. "I have been in this business long enough to know the unforeseen has a tendency to sneak up on one. Like your unusual cat, Sir Kahn."

Kim looked at Mr. Yoshida, knew his body was covered with tattoos under his silk shirt and tie.

"*Yakuza*, am I right?" Kim blurted out. Mr. Yamashita smiled at her.

"My friend John said you were very intelligent, capable."

He looked at John. "Unfortunately, and I think he will agree, too capable," he opined.

"You know, Mr. Yoshida, a Federal Agent, cannot just disappear without someone noticing."

"But of course, Ms. Kupar" replied the *Yakuza*. "However, we are intelligent also. So, my friend and partner, John, may have to disappear to temporarily, how do you say— Ah, fade the heat. I have always liked that expression. Reminds me of a swordsmith applying just the right heat to a *Katana*, then knowing when to squelch it, submerge it in cooling water."

"So you are partners in this-abortion?" Demanded Kim.

Mr. Yoshida frowned at her, then spoke. "This is strictly business. Although the commodities are often human and animal in nature. They are still just-commodities."

Kim barked out a laugh. "Commodities! Soon to include mutated and altered young women for 'jade eyes.' And beautiful Bengals. Like those in my country.

Turned into mutated monsters through genetic experimentation."

The Japanese Yakuza looked at John Wang. "She has not seen Sir Khan?" he asked.

"Not yet, my friend. I had hoped, at a later date- But, that plan is passed."

John looked at Kim.

"Monster, you say?" Asked John. "Let me show you a creation of beauty."

John yelled orders out in Mandarin, and a pair of Chinese voices answered affirmatively. Kim heard footsteps and movement.

"Boss, she hurt me," Samu spoke in Mandarin, sounded more like a petulant child than a full grown man.

"Kim, you hurt our Samu here?" Asked John in Mandarin, *"You saw his size, yes?"*

"Couldn't miss it. Samu smacked me first."

John frowned at Samu, spoke in a disapproving tone. *"Did I not say gently? Never mind. All is forgiven. But Kim, Samu here is one of our earliest projects with the human genome."*

"What are you saying, John?"

John smiled, then spoke. *"My Samu, tell my dear friend here how old you are."*

"I am fourteen."

Kim's mouth dropped open. Samu was at least two meters in height. He could easily be a poster child for the word "Huge" in Wikipedia.

"Surprised, Yes?" John now asked in English. "He is large, Kim. But he is no monster." John paused, pursed his lips, continued. "Although his mental development is a bit slow, at the bottom of the norm."

Just then Kim heard a cough she had not heard in quite some time. The unique cough of a Big Cat. Three Asian men pushed a humongous wheeled cage into the light. Even with the wheels, they were sweating and grunting as the good-sized Chinese pushed the cage into the light. Reclining as if he did not have a care in the world, was the biggest Bengal Kim had ever seen. She gasped exclaimed.

"My God! He is huge!"

John grinned before he replied. "But notice he is also well-formed, nor overweight as some mule Ligers and Tions are."

"Bring her closer, Samu. Let My Jade Beauty see another jade beauty," he ordered in Mandarin.

Samu walked her on her tiptoes to the cage. As they neared, Sir Khan's nose twitched. A scent caught, he was up in one smooth and quick motion, muzzle against the bars. Up close, Kim saw the huge saber teeth, the jade colored cat eyes above them, and her blood ran cold.

"You did it, you made a Saber Tooth Cat."

"But of course!" John exclaimed. "What better way to demonstrate our prowess with genetic manipulation? See, even his fur and hide are more tawny brown and black, with only a hint of striping."

John walked up close to Kim and the cage. "He's interested in something in your pocket." As he said that, Sir Khan reached a huge paw out through the bars, toward the targeted pocket.

"One moment, Sir Khan." John helped Samu to pull Kim back out of reach of the cage. He then reached into her pants pocket, found the item of interest.

"Ah, the famous tiger fur and claw key fob!"

Pronounced John. "From your Bengal victim." John held it out, and let the enormous cat to sniff it, out of reach of the paws. Kim was staring into Sir Kahn's eyes as he sniffed the object. Then human female and Sabre Tooth locked eyes.

Kim would claim something passed between the two. One a killer of a large cat, the other a large killer cat. They each saw and understood the other. Sir Kahn coughed, let out the hint of a deep growl that sounded almost like a purr. Then he reached his massive paw out through the cage bars again.

"Not yet, my furred friend," the Boss said. John motioned Samu to pull Kim back a bit further.

Kim glared at him. "So, he gets me. Correct?" she said with venom in her voice.

John let out a large sigh. "Perhaps. It may be up to you."

The 'Boss' motioned to the three Asians who had brought the cage in, one a Mongolian limo driver Kim had met before.

"Temur! Take those two, and bring our other guests in," the Chinese gangster ordered.

Mr. Yoshida walked up to Kim. "See?" he said. "Is not Sir Kahn magnificent?"

"You're in the animal smuggling business also?" Asked Kim.

He chuckled and replied. "I thought you understood. John and I are partners. He is the Public President. I am the Hidden President. If he must-disappear for a while, I'll run the operation until he returns. Then he returns under another identity. After all, so many of you Yankee Round Eyes- I'm sorry, you are far from that. So many Americans think all Asians look alike.

So, a nip here, tuck there, and he is new person."

"That's quite 'Western' of you. You forgot about fingerprints," Kim informed the *Yakuza*.

Now John laughed. "Prints are only as good as the database they are in. Some Chinese Cyberhacking and my prints belong to a new person."

Kim gave him a hard look. Then spoke. "You have this all figured out, don't you?"

Now John frowned. "Almost," he replied.

Two figures were dragged into the light, both struggling. Kim saw A.J, and Jade, much the worse for wear. Kim started to curse, move, but Samu clamped his unnaturally strong hands on her, held her tight, as Jade and A.J. were bound to two chairs.

"You just had to beat them, didn't you, Asshole!" Kim yelled at John Wang.

"I am sorry," he replied. "They tried to resist, even use some ancient pistol against my men. Here."

John Wang walked over to a table on the edge of the shadows, came back with the Howdah pistol."

"This is what you used to kill that Bengal you told me about, Yes?"

"Yes," Kim replied through angry, gritted teeth. If only she had not been so stupid, gotten caught-

"So, my Tiger Lady, what will it be?" Asked John. "You can cooperate, we hold Jade and A.J, as collateral. You help us work through all this severe government suspicion and inspection, then we let them go."

"What is to stop me from going to the authorities then?" Kim questioned her former lover.

"As with my records," answered the crime boss, "we could easily manipulate certain databases to make it appear you were a participant in this whole enterprise from the beginning. After all, you have expertise in Big Cats. A tweak here and there, and you are also a criminal mastermind in exotic animal smuggling."

John stared at her, then spoke. "Who would believe you then?"

Kim looked at him, her mind racing. What to do, what to do!

A.J. yelled out in Punjabi through bloodied lips. *"No deal, Big Sister! They'll kill us all anyway!"*

One of the Chinese men hit him hard in the stomach, and he partially bent over.

John frowned. "All you Kupars are tough and stubborn," he observed. "Right now, those are not attractive traits, unlike your jade eyes."

Kim tried to stall, hoped something unforeseen would happen.

"So I'm to trust that the Chinese Triad, the Yakuza, and Vietnamese street gangs will all keep a bargain, keep me and mine safe?"

"Yes. You'll have our word."

Kim exploded into laughter. "Your word?" she spat out. "Like your word that you loved me? Would protect me? All Lies. Do I have a big red 'S' written on my face for 'stupid'? You lying piece of pigshit!" Then she tried to spit at him, for her genuine anger and hurt were now overflowing.

John Wang's face blanched, then flushed with anger as he spoke.

"You stupid cunt. We could have had it all. ALL! But you just had to be a vaunted Federal Agent. Meddling in a Man's World. "

John looked at Mr. Yoshida. "It is over," he stated. "I will dispose of the bodies. And we will use the contingency plan."

Mr. Yoshida stepped up, shook John Wang's hand with a slight bow. "I am sorry, my friend. True love is hard to find."

"But this business—" John paused. "I again must make a sacrifice. However, I knew that when I began, there would be sacrifices. Like your associate's missing finger. A sacrifice to make things right, and for our honor."

"Honor?" Kim spoke snorted. "Yes, real honor. Killing women, the innocent."

John turned toward the Vietnamese gang members. "Now you will earn your positions. Dispose of those two," he commanded.

Mr. Yoshida slowly shook his head. "I fear, Ms. Kupar, that you and your fellows will never understand," the *Yakuza* boss said. "All Asians can work together, forget ancient hatreds and feuds."

"And feed people to giant cats. Real great Pan Asian Partnership."

"I think, friend John," the Japanese man said, "that she may be too tough and full of bile to feed—"

A report of a large caliber weapon echoed through the basement area. Everyone froze in place.

John Wang grabbed his cell phone, punched in a number. As he waited for an answer, there was another loud report. Then another. John cursed.

"Temur! All you others! Someone has breached the doorway from upstairs, the guards are dead or gone. Take your weapons, stop *whoever is here.*"

"*Samu, in five minutes, give Kim to Sir Kahn,*" John commanded in Mandarin, "*then the other two.*"

"*Yes, Boss.*"

John Wang retrieved Kim's pistols that Samu had taken from her. He handed the Sig Sauer to Mr. Yoshida as he spoke.

"Here, a forty caliber. And a small Glock 26 for your associate."

Mr. Yoshida spoke Japanese to his younger associate, who produced a short Ninja style sword from under his suit jacket.

"He prefers cold steel."

"Suit yourself," the Boss said. "Come on. We must deal quickly with whoever is attacking us."

"Maybe a rival gang, John?" Yoshida asked.

"I only heard one weapon," he replied to his fellow criminal, "so I don't know. Hurry."

All the criminal elements moved across the long-hidden basement toward the far end and the concealed stairway leading upstairs.

In the lighted area, Kim, A.J. and Jade remained. With Samu and Sir Khan.

Samu looked down at Kim.

"You kicked me," Samu spoke almost like a child in Chinese.

"Sorry, Big Man. Did not know who you were."

"Samu!" Jade yelled from across the room. *"Let us go! Please!"*

Samu looked toward Jade. *"You were always nice to me,"* the huge man-boy said.

He looked down at Kim. *"You weren't. You go to Sir Kahn."*

The man-boy picked her up by her arms, moved toward the oversized cage. Samu spoke to Sir Kahn in Mandarin as he suspended Kim by holding her wrists in his massive hand, as effective as any metal clamp.

"Nice little cat. Samu has another playmate for you—" He began to slide open the bolt to the cage door with his free hand.

Kim exploded into action.

Samu had forgotten how painful her kicks were until Kim planted both her feet together into his face. He howled in pain from a broken nose and dropped Kim. The Special Agent hit the ground as sounds of a full-blown firefight echoed through the basement. She spun to meet the attack of the man-boy. He was still holding his broken nose.

"You hurt my nose!!" He looked up, screamed, and charged.

Kim managed to evade his grasping meat-hook hands, kicked at his legs. Samu stumbled into the cage, turned around fast for someone of his bulk, and charged again. Kim drove her right foot into his groin as hard as she could. Samu's eyes bugged out, and he dropped to his knees as Kim scrambled backward. Samu began to sob.

Kim saw a chance and took it. She dashed to A.J. and Jade's sides. Kim bent over and retrieved s small slim piece of metal from her sock.

"What's that?" A.J. asked.

"Razorblade. Trick T-Rex taught me." She began to saw at A.J.s bindings, managed to free his hands. She handed the razor blade to him.

"Cut your legs loose, then Jade."

Kim spun around, ran past to the table on the shadow's edge.

"Bingo." The Howdah pistol was still there. A.J. had not gotten a shot off, which told her the minions had used John's copy of her key to get in (Stupid!) and surprise him and Jade.

Huge hands grabbed her from the rear, lifted her up like a rag doll.

"You hurt me!" Blood flowed down Samu's face. Kim tried to bring the large double-barreled pistol to bear.

There was a roar, and something bigger than even Samu slammed into him, sent Kim flying across the room. She managed to use a martial art break-fall and roll, staggered to her feet, Howdah still in hand. A scream came from the shadows, was cut off. Then she heard horrible and loud crunching sounds.

Sir Kahn was loose.

"O God, O God, O God—" she repeated to herself as she tried to move as quick and quiet as she could to A. J. and Jade. A.J. was slashing Jade's bindings as fast as he could. Kim whispered, "Hurry, but quiet," then turned toward where Sir Kahn had gone. The Howdah pistol shook in her hands. Would it be big enough for this massive beast of a Sabre Tooth Cat?

Then she heard a loud and familiar voice. *"Raptor! T-Rex is here!"*

She smiled, blinked back tears. Damn, crazy, lovable fool. Came alone like some old Western hero. Which could get them both killed.

More shooting and Kim dared not cry out for fear of attracting Sir Kahn's attention. She motioned to the now freed Jade and A.J. to follow her as she tried to get her bearings in this dark basement. Jade pointed a direction.

"There, Kim. There is a small stairwell up to the Wang's private office."

"Okay. Quietly now. Sir Kahn is a hunting cat."

"He is more," Jade whispered. "He is as smart as you or I."

Kim looked at her. "Made that way?" she asked.

Jade nodded her head, spoke. "Yes."

"That's great," whispered A.J.

"Come on," said Kim. "Time to leave."

The three made their way through the dim light, hearing cursing, and cries of pain from the other side of the hidden basement. Then more shots as the firefight began anew. Bullets zipped overhead, ricocheted nearby. Kim could not tell who was who in the darkness. At least the shooting meant that Rex was still alive. They all crouched as low as possible as they tried not to be shot.

In the dim light, a figure approached. Kim brought up the Howdah pistol, pointed it at the possible threat. Then a voice broke the silence.

"Raptor?" It was Rex.

Kim tried not to laugh for joy. "T-Rex, you old fool," she whispered. "I didn't think you would come alone when I texted you."

"Had to," he answered. "It would've taken me hours to get the bureaucracy moving. There is no time. Plus I thought you would wait for me."

Kim looked at Rex's rifle. "That is not government issue."

"FN-FAL .308 battle rifle. Ex-Indian. Your people used them," the Senior Agent replied.

Kim pointed to the small stairway to John Wang's office. "There. Exit to upstairs."

"Got it. Move," T-Rex ordered.

Bullets whizzed by at the same time as there were loud and close gunshots and muzzle flashes. T-Rex staggered into Kim, tried to remain standing. The female

Agent shoved him toward A.J., brought the Howdah tiger pistol up two-handed and fired a barrel at the attackers. There was a loud report, bright muzzle flash as the black-powder weapon sent a heavy load of buckshot fanning out into the basement. Kim was greeted with screams of pain as some of the buckshot found targets.

She grabbed an arm of T-Rex, began to pull him along. The older Agent pushed her away. "I'm okay. Rounds hit my tactical body armor. Bruised only."

Kim yelled at A.J. and Jade, there was no reason to be quiet now. "Move!" The two young people did not have to be told twice. They dashed to the stairway, followed by Kim and T-Rex. A.J. paused at the bottom of the stairs.

"Kim—"

"Up. This is my job, not yours, Little Brother."

T-Rex shoved a pistol at her brother as he spoke. "Glock 26. Point and shoot."

"Got it. You get my Sister—"

"My Partner's getting out with me. Move!" T-Rex ordered.

A.J. looked at Kim, then began clambering up the narrow stairs with Jade.

T-Rex swapped magazines in his rifle, then grabbed at another pocket in his tactical vest.

"Here. My Sig…"

A loud report and a heavy slug struck T-Rex. He went down. Kim screamed in anger, fired the remaining barrel of the Howdah at the threat. Again, a loud scream of pain as the buckshot hit a minion. Kim crouched next to her partner.

"Rex! T-Rex. Say something!"

"Vest did not stop that one," he grunted out. "Must be an AP round. Shit." He began to slump a little. Kim dropped the empty Howdah, grabbed at the Sig Sauer T-Rex had been trying to hand her.

"*Stop right there, Kim.*" The words were in Mandarin. It was John Wang. Kim slowly turned her head, to see him in the dim light.

"*Take your hand off the pistol, my love. I still don't want to shoot you.*"

"*You expect me to let you kill my partner, my friend?*" Kim asked in Mandarin.

John took a step closer. He had a chrome plated Tokarev pistol pointed at her. "*I can help save him. I will use him as collateral for your continued silence. Or he can die. Your choice.*"

Kim weighed the chances of spinning around and shooting him with the Sig Sauer.

"*You know, John, someone must have heard all the shooting,*" Kim suggested.

John Wang smiled as he spoke. "*Not really. The basement is soundproofed. I did that for special occasions.*"

"*Like when you have a large tiger beast prowling around?*"

"*That, and dealing with problems of a human nature. Now. Hand off the pistol. Or I will shoot T-Rex also. Again, your choice.*"

Kim slowly stood, looked directly into John's eyes.

"*Why not just shoot me, no choices?*" Kim asked.

"*Because, you silly fool, I DO love you!*" John announced. "*That is not a lie. A weakness, but not a lie.*"

Kim saw in John' eyes and face that it was true. Yet she knew that even the most potent love could not change the reality that John was a force for Evil. Kim could not ever live with that.

"Then you have a problem, John Wang, President of the Seattle Asian Business Association," the Special Agent responded. "For I must arrest you for all your crimes. That is my job, my calling. My honor."

John began to curse. "Damn You! We could have had it all! Power, money, a family!"

"No, John," Kim stated. "Not based on lies. And death."

Even in the dim light, Kim could see John's face was flushed and screwed up with anger as he cried out.

"Just too damned smart for your own good. Now, I must do this. For, I answer to others in China, where my family still lives."

Kim stood tall, straight. A calmness came over here as she knew her fate was near. But at least A.J. and Jade had fled. They would tell the true story.

"Goodbye then, John."

John sputtered something unintelligible.

T-Rex picked that moment to start speaking from the basement floor.

"Tiger, Tiger, burning bright,
 In the forests of the night,
 What immortal hand or eye,
 Could frame thy fearful symmetry?"

Surprised, both Kim and John Wang looked at him.

"What are you—" John began. Then Kim noticed T-Rex was looking past her and John, into the basement. Two large eyes shone among the darkness. She gasped.

John Wang realized something was behind him. With widened eyes, he tried to turn around. A colossal shape sprang from the darkness, sending his pistol spinning toward Kim. The form drove him into the darkness, where he screamed. Once. Kim heard a loud crunching and snapping sound. Then silence.

Kim unfroze herself, reached for chrome Tokarev near her feet. Then she heard that cough. Slowly, Kim straightened up, stared into the eyes of Death.

"Sir Kahn", she whispered at the creature whose face was mere inches from her face. She closed her eyes, waited for the inevitable permanent blackness.

A loud snuffle and the huge Sabre Tooth Cat/Tiger was gone into the darkness of the basement.

Kim opened her eyes, began to shake. Then a voice cut in.

"Hey, Raptor, down here. I'm leaking."

Kim jerked her attention to T-Rex on the floor. Now she could notice a widening pool of blood. She began to cry as she ripped her shirt apart, tried to make a crude bandage to stem the flow of blood from a nasty wound. T-Rex had been holding his hand over a sucking chest wound, using a fold in his body armor in an attempt to keep his perforated lung form sucking air in through the bullet hole, and then collapsing.

"First Aid Kit. My belt—" T-Rex coughed out.

Kim found it, pulled a small plastic card that made a good seal over the lung wound. She tried to wrap a bandage around it, pulling at T-Rex's body armor.

"No time," gasped T-Rex. "Get out. Call for help."

"Go to Hell, you old fart! You're my goddamned partner!" Kim raged. "You're coming with me."

"Other bad guys around—"

"I have John's pistol," declared Kim. She looked at the grip, saw the bright red star. Red Star Import Export.

How was she so blind?

A human figure charged from the darkness. Mr. Yamashita's unnamed associate had his short Ninja sword raised in his one good arm. Kim rolled back, brought the Tokarev up to fire.

A series of rapid-fire shots came from up the hidden office stairs, knocked the attacker over. Kim looked up. It was Jade, with the Glock.

"How—"

"Point and shoot your friend said. Simple." The Chinese woman's jade colored eyes had a steely quality that Kim had not seen before as she replied.

"Where is A.J.?" Kim asked.

"He took a pistol from a dead man upstairs, went down the street to find the Police. He said he'd fire off some bullets to get attention if need be."

"My type of guy," T-Rex managed to rasp out.

"Don't talk, Rex. Here, try to stand up—"

Kim, with Jade's help, managed to get the beefy man to his feet. They began to climb the stairs.

"You shot the men upstairs, T-Rex," Kim stated.

"Ask me no questions, tell you no lies," T-Rex managed to croak out.

"I said, don't talk. God, you are stubborn."

"That's why... you like me." He stumbled on the stairs, gasped out, "Need to sit for a moment—"

"Don't you dare die on me, you old dinosaur! You got that?" Kim commanded

Rex slumped to the steps but gave Kim a wry smile as he mumbled, "Never, Raptor. You're stuck with me." Then he passed out.

30.

Kim made her way to the private hospital room that was Rex Moyer's home for the foreseeable future. She had a small bouquet of flowers that she knew he would reject as not being 'manly,' but she did not care. The Agent also had a funny 'get well card' that had some Dinosaurs on the outside and inside. A concealed mocha coffee rounded out her items she'd collected for her T-Rex.

A.J. had gotten there with the 'Calvary' moments after T-Rex had collapsed on the stairs. It had been touch and go after that, as the armor piercing bullet of Chinese manufacture had barely missed his heart. A few millimeters closer- She stopped herself from going there. The important thing was he was alive. Everything else, any problems she may have, were secondary. She smiled. Even the fact there was a huge manufactured Sabre Tooth Cat still missing seemed so unimportant. Her Partner was alive. Everything and everyone else could take a long jump off a short pier. Which included people investigating her and Rex for the incident.

Dave Keegan had magically shown up after the 'Jade Palace Shootout' hit the overnight news media. Kim had looked at him at askance. Dave could see the suspicion in her face.

"Let me guess. John Wang was a client, so you think I am part of this whole thing," declared Dave.

"Why shouldn't I? He had you on retainer."

Dave paused, shook his head as he replied. "Well, I guess I have to expect that. But my heart is still Blue. So Law Enforcement Officers come first. Not to mention, I would not dishonor the service of my friends, like Rex."

Kim tried to look into his soul. Dave had a record of exemplary service in the Border Patrol and Homeland Security Investigations. Plus, Rex trusted him... a lot. She sighed.

"I guess if T-Rex trusts you, Raptor should also," said Kim

"Raptor??" Dave asked.

"That's my 'handle,' I was told. Rex also said to me if I complained too much about it, I'd be given a worse one."

Dave smiled and said. "I guess it fits. He told me you kicked ass."

"Well, I was getting my butt kicked until T-Rex showed up," Kim admitted. "He saved me."

"And you saved him. That's what Partners do," the former Special Agent explained. "Now, let's see about covering your collective rear ends. Start from the beginning—"

Her mind back in the present, Kim checked in with the Ward Nurse, then walked down to Rex's room. As she neared, she heard familiar voices. She knocked and entered the room, found Jade and A.J. sitting next to his bed.

"Look what the cat drug in," Rex said.

Kim cringed a bit. "The word 'cat' is going to have a special meaning to me for a while. At least until Sir Kahn is found."

"Hey, Kim. Not your problem," Rex informed her. "Besides, an animal that size will have trouble hiding for long."

"Well, as the resident 'Tiger Lady' I can tell you that normal Bengals are notorious for hiding in almost plain sight in India," she explained. "So, it may be a while. But let's change the subject to why I'm here. How are you, Rex?"

Rex snorted and grumbled. "I'd be doing lot better if I could get out of here. I'm trying to get A.J. and Jade to smuggle some beer or something in—"

"How about a mocha coffee?" Kim interjected.

Rex grinned and answered. "Ah, I knew there was a reason why I like you. Gimmee."

Kim handed him the coffee. Rex glanced at the door, looking for a nurse to come in and confiscate it. When none showed, he took a large slurp.

"Ah. Elixir of the Gods."

Kim grinned. "I thought that was Scotch," she said

"That too, my dear," admitted Rex. "Now, find a seat—"

"We were just leaving," interrupted A.J. "You can have my seat."

"Hey, I don't want to chase you off, Little Brother," protested Kim.

Jade stood up. "We have thanked our T-Rex here, for coming to our aid. Now…" The young Chinese woman with the jade eyes stepped up to Kim and hugged her. She whispered in Mandarin into her ear.

"*Thank you, dear one, for saving me and my new found love.*"

"*You do love my brother, don't you?*" Kim whispered back.

"*Yes, with all my heart.*"

Kim fought back the lump in her throat, the tears in her eyes. At least someone had found true love. She knew her brother would take care of Jade, would be loyal. That was a family trait, to a fault.

A.J. Walked up and hugged her also. "We'll go out to dinner, sometimes Our Father is helping us find new jobs, what with Jade Palace being closed down," he explained.

"Well, maybe the legitimate Indian Tribes that John Wang was dealing with will step forward with some new investors," Kim suggested.

A.J. shrugged and answered. "I'll take what I can get. I have a new responsibility now." He looked at Jade, who latched on to his arm.

"I will also go back to school," said Jade. "I want to be a veterinarian, to help lost and abused animals. Like Sir Kahn."

Kim looked at Jade. "You see him as a victim?" she asked.

Jade nodded. "He didn't ask to be made that way. John Wang made him that way, stopped him from ever being a normal Bengal. He's alone now." She looked up at A.J., hugged his arm tighter as she added, "I am not. We all need love, family."

Kim felt the pang of new loneliness again. To be so close, to think that she had found her true love-then have it become evil, almost kill her. She shook the feeling off, forced a smile at A.J. and Jade.

"Yes," Kim agreed. "You are wise beyond your years. I wish you all the happiness there is."

The two young lovers grinned, kissed. "See you later, Big Sister," A.J. said

"You've got that right. Little Brother," replied Kim.

The couple left, and Kim stood alone for a moment, staring into space.

"Well, when you are finished ruminating, Kim, I could use some help adjusting this dammable bed," grumbled Rex.

"Oh, sorry. Overthinking."

"I had supervisors who wished I did more of that," he added

Kim smiled and walked to the bedside.

"Try adjusting the back of the bed, raising it," instructed Rex.

Kim bent over. Rex gave you a quick kiss on the cheek.

"Thanks."

"What was that for?" Kim sputtered out.

"I know, sexual harassment and all that. But I'm just trying to... " His mouth moved, nothing came out.

"What? My God, are you tongue-tied?" Kim asked.

Rex stayed sitting up in his bed, seemed to be trying to form words.

"Hey, say something!" The female Agent demanded. "Are you having a stroke?"

A tear ran down his cheek. "Goddammit. I told

myself I wouldn't cry."

Kim grabbed his arm and asked. "What's wrong, T-Rex? Your Raptor is here. After all, we've been through—"

More tears came as the 'dinosaur Agent' croaked out. "Thank You for saving me. Thank you for being alive. If you had died—"

Kim hugged him and whispered. "Hey, you told me that's what Partners do. Dave Keegan said the same."

"I never had a female partner before. Never had a woman-save my ass. Other than my wife Lynn," he added. "She helped save my soul."

Kim stepped back, looked at this 'tough guy' who was dealing with a flood of emotions after almost dying. And worried about how it looked to others. She realized that for all his braggadocio, Rex Moyer had never been this close to his own death, had to deal with his own mortality. Then to have the traditional roles reversed and the woman he was supposed to save, saved him? He was shaken more to his core than he wanted to admit.

Kim squeezed his arm, grabbed some tissues, and handed them to him.

"Here. Your mascara will run," she advised.

Rex wiped his eyes, then blew his nose.

"Thanks. Don't tell anyone—"

"That I saw you cry? Don't worry," Kim admitted. "You're Mr. Macho is safe."

Kim took a deep breath, let it out to speak. "Now, it's my turn. *You* saved *my* ass, in your words. You showed up, no questions asked. Even after I disregarded some of your warnings about John Wang. I was stupid, with stars in my eyes, all wrapped up with being 'in love,' and ignored suspicions I had, even about Jade. If you hadn't shown up—"

Now it was her turn to be teary-eyed. She grabbed some tissues, dabbed at her eyes.

"Just a couple of weak softies, aren't we?" Kim stated.

Rex gazed at her. "Raptor, you and T-Rex are never weak," he declared. "We make one helluva team. The young and smart, the old and stubborn. In the palaver of West Texas, put her there, Pard."

Rex stuck his hand out, and she grasped it. T-Rex was like a 'Dutch Uncle,' or just a true related uncle, like her Uncle Abe. Uncles helped to hold extended families together. Kim was glad she had now an adopted one.

"Knock knock." It was a female voice. In walked a slender blonde.

"Hey, Babe. Kim, this is my wife Lynn. Came to make sure I'm not molesting the nurses."

The older woman laughed with a pleasant sing-song voice. She walked up to Kim.

"So you're my husband's young partner. He's talked a lot about you," she said.

"Well, Ma'am, he talks a lot about you."

"Probably complaining about the problems I caused him over the years," the wife opined.

"Babe! Now don't start—" warned Rex.

Lynn reached out and pulled Kim to her in a hug, said, "Kim Kupar, thanks for getting the love of my life out of that Hell Hole. I owe you."

"Ma'am, he was there because of ME," Kim protested.

The wife released the hug, looked Kim in her eyes as she continued. "No, he was there because he has always been a hard charger, racing into harm's way. It finally caught up with him." Lynn looked over at her husband.

"Are you finally ready to retire?" she asked.

"Mandatory, in less than a year. Thought I'd last it out," Rex said.

"Oh, really? Agent Kupar, if he stays in, can you keep him out of trouble?" Lynn asked

"Ma'am—"

"Kim, that's Lynn. Ma'am was my mother. Now, he says you have been helping keep him on the straight and narrow. Can you still do it?" Questioned Lynn.

Kim saw an older married couple with children who were comfortable with their relationship, we're now a lot alike. Plus, Rex apparently was taking any problems Kim had caused onto his own back as if she were a daughter or a niece. Kim glanced at Rex and saw a quick wink.

"If they let me, Lynn," agreed Kim. "Yes."

Lynn smiled and said. "Good. Now I know I have somebody trying to keep my hard headed husband out of trouble. Sorry I did not get a chance to meet you at Matt Swenson's funeral. But, at least now we have that remedied."

"Hoping to get out of here tomorrow, Babe," Rex interjected.

"Oh no, you don't!" Exclaimed Lynn. "You're staying here as long as I can convince the hospital to hold you. Let them deal with Grumpy Bear."

Rex winced. Kim smiled, then grinned.

"Grumpy Bear?" she asked

"Oh I see, He never mentioned that nickname," Lynn said. "I can see I have a lot to tell you over coffee someday. Like the time—"

A new voice was heard. "Is this Agent Moyer's-oh daughter! There you are."

Kim looked up and saw her father and mother standing in the doorway.

"Mother, Father! What are you doing here!"

"This is your father?" Rex asked from his bed. "Sir, anybody ever tell you that you raise one tough lady?"

A smile threatened at the corners of Balraj Singh Kupar's mouth. "If you mean stubborn, I will agree."

"*Father...*" said Kim in Punjabi. Her mother stepped forward toward Rex and his wife.

"You must be Rex, T-Rex. Husband, the box."

"Yes, dear."

Kim's mother stepped forward and stated, "I'm Guadalupe, her mother. This is my husband, Balraj."

"Pleased to meet you both. This is my wife, Lynn."

Guadalupe and Lynn shook hands.

"Very pleased to meet you, Guadalupe. You must be very proud of your daughter."

Guadalupe stood a bit straighter, clearly showing her pride, as she spoke. "Yes, she is a fine young woman. Now if I could find a decent husband for her..."

"Mother!" Kim cried out.

Rex began to laugh. Guadalupe looked at him and asked, "Do you have any available sons, other young men—"

"Mother. Please." Kim began to blush.

"Guadalupe, dear. That is not why we are here," Balraj reminded his wife.

"It never hurts to ask. But you're right," Kim's mother agreed as she spoke at Rex.

"My husband has something for you for protecting our daughter and son, A.J."

"Hey, I was just doing my job," protested Rex. "Besides, we can't accept gifts…"

"Cultural exchange, Rex. Remember?" Kim smiled as she said it. Her father stepped forward, bowed.

"Please accept this as a token of our great appreciation for you efforts in keeping our only daughter safe," he stated. "And for helping our son."

Rex tried not to blush, accepted the wooden box. He looked at it, then removed the lid.

"Well, I be damned… is this what I think it is?" Rex asked with a bit of wonder.

Kim stepped up and looked into the box. And gasped.

"Father. Is that—"

"That is a Sikh dagger, a *Kirpan*. Handed down in my family for generations," Balraj acknowledged.

Rex stuttered a bit, then said "I can't accept this. I am not Sikh."

"But you perform one of the tenants of our Guru," said Kim's father. "You protect the oppressed, the persecuted. Are not victims of Human Trafficking oppressed and persecuted?? "

Rex looked at Kim, who gave a slight nod. Rex reverently put the dagger back in the box

"Sir, I am honored beyond words," declared Rex.

"My husband, speechless?" Lynn interjected. "This is a first. I'll have to mark this day down."

Guadalupe laughed, then added, "You will have to both come over for dinner after your husband is out of the hospital."

"Why, that would be nice. Then I'll return the invitation."

Guadalupe walked over, linked arms with Lynn.

"Come, I'll buy you some coffee," she told the other wife. "Then we can exchange notes on our children and husbands."

"Good," replied Lynn. "Rex, I'll be back later. You relax, okay."

"Sure, Babe," he replied. "See you in a bit."

As the two wives walked toward the cafeteria, Balraj stepped over to his daughter and spoke.

"Now, Daughter, I have something for you." "What is that, Father?" Kim asked.

The dark skinned man embraced Kim, kissed her. "Your Mother says I do not tell you how proud I am of you. From this day forward, I will. I'll tell everyone. For a man could not have a better daughter. I love you, Kimberly. Never forget that," he said as he began to choke up.

Kim tried to blink back tears, but could not. "I love you too, Father. Thank You."

They stayed embraced for a while, then parted. "I must join your Mother, so she does not get you married off before you leave," Balraj advised his daughter.

Kim laughed as she wiped away tears. "Yes. She'll try that, won't she?" Kim replied.

"Always follow your head and heart, Kim," advised her father. "You will find the right person. I did. As have both your brothers."

"Thank You, Father."

Balraj looked at Rex. "Come see us when you are better, T-Rex," he offered the Senior Agent. "You are welcome in our home at any time."

"Thank you again, Sir. I will."

Rex and Kim were quiet for a while after he father left. Rex broke the silence.

"Your father is a wise man."

"I Know. So are you," stated Kim.

"What have you been smoking, Agent? Wacky Tobacky? Me, wise? Just ask my wife," advised Rex.

Kim smiled and added, "She thinks you are wise. I can tell. Just ask her. And she loves you."

Rex grunted. "Yeah, I know," he agreed. "I just wonder why at times. But like they say, never look a gift horse in the mouth. And never accept gifts from Greeks. They'll get you every time."

Kim laughed. "Time to go," she said. "But I guess I'll see you in work soon."

"Just as soon as I can," declared Rex. "This place is driving me nuts."

Kim stepped over to his bedside and kissed his cheek. "You hang in there, my Dutch Uncle."

"Keep your powder dry, Raptor."

Kim smiled, then walked down the hall.

She knew there would still be some questions as to what exactly happened at the Jade Palace. Especially when Sir Kahn was caught. Right now, the news outlets had statements and headlines about 'Two Federal Agents Save Human Trafficking Victims,' and 'Shootout! Homeland Security Agents Win Gunfight.' Little was mentioned about a missing tiger. But the smart Sabre Tooth Cat was out there. Kim hoped there were no more human victims. A headless corpse was identified as Mr. Yoshida, which raised Sir Kahn's number of victims to three at least.

As Kim walked out of the hospital lobby, she saw three familiar faces. Alan White, Kregg Sorenson and Hank Thomas. Alan hailed her.

"You see T-Rex?"

"Yes. He is as ornery as ever."

"Well," added Kregg. "Us Veterans have to stick together. I'm going to sneak a small bottle in for him. He says he needs a shot."

Kim grinned. Then she looked at Hank. "You seeing him also?" she asked.

Hank shrugged and said, "Yeah. He's good people. Like you."

Kregg must have caught the vibes between the two, as he said to Alan. "Let's get some coffee before we go up. See you up there, Hank."

"Yeah."

Alan and Kregg walked away, as Kim and Hank stood in an awkward silence. Then they both tried to talk at once.

"Do you," "How About," They both stopped, looked at each other. Then laughed.

"Feels like a scene in an old romantic comedy, Kim."

"Yeah," she agreed. "Or some Bollywood soap opera."

Their eyes met. "Want to get something to eat, Hank?" Kim asked.

"Yeah. Sure," agreed Hank. "What do you feel like?"

Kim chuckled as she said. "Anything but Chinese."

Hank tried not to laugh but failed. Kim joined in. About a minute later, they stopped.

"Let's blow this joint, Tiger Lady."

Kim grinned reached over and grabbed his hand. The feel of his firm grip started some old familiar butterflies in her stomach.

This time she did not clamp them down.

31.

WEST END, TACOMA NARROWS BRIDGE

The shifting of something substantial in the back of his semi-truck trailer, plus some banging so loud he could hear it in the truck cab, caused Mike West to pull his rig over to a side lane shoulder a football field past the end of the Tacoma Narrows Bridge. He began to curse, something he had become quite good at in the Army. He been the military equivalent of a 'Teamster' during his active duty, some of it overseas. He saw no reason not to use these acquired skills once he got off Active Duty.

After he stopped and exited the rig, he saw a Washington State Trooper vehicle pull over behind his truck, its wig wags, and overhead emergency lights flashing.

"Ah shit," he said. All he needed was another ticket for load weight variance, a log book problem, or some other expensive violation to really screw up his week. He slowed his walk to the back of the truck, trying to see if he recognized the Trooper in the dimming light of sunset.

"Good evening Sir... oops, I mean, Ma'am." For the Trooper was a young Susan Etheridge, a female just off probation as a road officer. He had met her a couple times before, once at the weigh station. She seemed nice enough, not a hard ass. And, the added plus was her five foot eight physique was VERY nice to look at, even in a State Trooper Uniform.

Trooper Etheridge walked up to West, gave him a slight smile as she spoke.

"Good Evening. I think we've met before. Anything wrong?"

"To be honest, my load seems to be shifting," Mike answered. "Something seems to have broken loose or... something. I can feel it, and hear a racket in the cab."

Trooper Etheridge frowned. "No livestock, animals in there? I know this is not a cattle trailer, but, well, people sometimes try to move some odd things in the wrong type of trailer."

"Yes, Ma'am," the Teamster answered. "I watched them load the crates and stuff, and it looked like they had the trailer packed pretty good. But... Hell, all I know is, something is weird."

The Trooper walked over, saw he had a lock on the tall trailer door. "Yours?" she asked

"Yes, Ma'am. Got the key right here."

"Okay. Open her up, we'll take a look. Then I'll need to see your log book, license, registration, and insurance," the Trooper advised. "And your load manifests."

"Of course," Mike replied as he went to open the large back door and swing it open. With practiced ease, he had it unlocked and was opening it when he heard a loud roar, then was knocked flat on his ass as something slammed into the door. The Trooper let out a combination of a squeal and a cry, as she back peddled and pulled her service pistol. A oversized dark shape disappeared into the dusk light alongside the highway.

"What the fuck was THAT?" Mike yelled out.

"I don't know-you okay?" The Trooper cried out.

"Yes, Ma'am. Just knocked on my ass."

"It looked like some zoo... oh, shit." The trooper stopped what she was going to say, turned and hurried back to her Prowler. Mike scrambled up and followed. The Trooper pulled an oversized flyer out, with a large photo of a tiger on it.

"My God. That's it. An escaped tiger!" The Trooper declared.

"What?" Asked Mike. "How did that get into MY rig?"

"I have no idea. But you'll have to stay here," the young Trooper advised Mike." There'll be some Federal Agents coming to check out your load, collect some forensics."

Mike cursed some more, began to create new swear words beyond the means of normal mortal men. Even Susan Etheridge was impressed by his unique command of the English language. He ended his rant with a plaintive "Why me? Why does it have to be ME?"

The Man created Sabre Tooth Cat known as Sir Kahn looked from the shadows back toward the human machine it had traveled in. As he watched the male and female humans scurry around, his enhanced intelligence told it that more of the large, upright monkeys would soon come. Time to move further from the Puget Sound. As Sir Kahn swiftly and silently made his way into and up the Kitsap Peninsula, the considerable feline's enhanced senses caught the scent of a large female cat which was in season, in 'heat.' The native Cougar was not a Bengal, but then neither was Sir Khan, really. So, the female Cougar would do to satisfy its lust for 'love' and procreation.

The African Lion gene splices had made Sir Kahn much more social than the solitary Bengals. Thus he would look for the 'special one' of the opposite gender to satisfy all his desires. At the same time, a part of Sir Kahn's brain processed the memory of the Tiger Lady human. The presence of that female was unique. Would he see her again?

A stronger scent of the in-season female feline made Sir Kahn concentrate on the mission at hand. He moved faster in the forests of Western Washington, his unique fur blending in with the new surroundings. Other woodland creatures scurried away as this new apex predator slid through the brush. They could not know that Sir Kahn was not looking for food prey. Instead, he searched for something more important to some creatures.

Sir Kahn looked for Love.

Made in United States
Troutdale, OR
10/21/2023

13900104R00159